SNATCH

The Adventures of David and Me in Old New York

Volume 1

A Novella

Charles Fuller

David and Me Publishing Inc.
P.O. Box 30443
Philadelphia, PA 19130
www.davidandmeinnyc.com

Cover and interior book design by 1106 Design

Second Printing

ISBN: 978-0-9845846-1-1

*For my two sons Charles III and David Ira Fuller,
and my wife Claire Prieto-Fuller
whose love and hard work made what you are
holding in your hands a reality.*

CHAPTER ONE

September 4, 1838

MY FLOAT WAS BOBBING UP and down in the Hudson River like something was trying to pull it under. I grabbed my fishing pole, thinking I had snared, at the very least, a three or four pound striped bass. Sadly, all that was on my hook was a dirty canvas bag partially covered in mud. Small and soaked clear through, it was a gray thing, with a leather drawstring around the top of it.

"What is it?" David reached for it.

I yanked it away and opened it. 'Course, David grumbled—he always grumbles. The first law of fishing is you get first dibs at whatever winds up on *your hook*. Inside the bag was a leather belt with the initials B.C. cut in the tip, and a folded piece of paper with what looked like the word, *Alabam* scribbled on it. I hadn't paid much attention to the outside of the bag. When I scraped away the mud I realized there was a faded image of a skull on one side. A skull with horns on both sides of its forehead and a smile that made it seem as though it was about to speak. I had seen the smiling skull's head before, drawn in chalk on the front door of a burned-out house on Little Water Street. It was the sign of the 'New York Kidnapping Club',[1] a notorious group of men and a few women, white and black, led by the mysterious Snatch, who helped agents return 'fugitive slaves', runaways or unsuspecting freemen caught on the streets of New York, to the slave states of the South.[2]

"What does that mean?" David pointed to the skull.

"Something awful," I said. Seeing that image made me shudder. As far as I was concerned it was time to head home. The sun was setting over New Jersey anyway, and the low slung clouds fanning its final red-orange rays signaled that time of day when dusk could easily turn to danger.

Just as I was about to pick up my pole, I saw him out the corner of my eye. A tall, young, black seaman, cast a long angular shadow on the wall of the warehouse as he moved behind a row of empty barrels. I almost missed him. When I opened the water-logged bag, my left hand started itching, a sure sign something unexpected would happen. I was ready to run, but David had seen him too. *Curious* is the best word to describe my ten-year-old brother. With no regard for the bluegill he had just caught, his line, or pole, David began walking in the man's direction.

"Where are you goin'?"

"He could be hurt Charlie, I think he fell down!" The man seemed to slide down the wall, more than fall. He was breathing heavily when David reached him. "What's the matta', Sir?"

David was always polite. Me? I was remembering that Snatch was said to be a master of disguise who loved grabbing gullible children. If it was Snatch, he was bound to get one of us—and I could always out-run David! Though the consequence of arriving home without him, while not as horrific as being sold into slavery, could well leave scars I'd remember for a life-time. Our dad would kill me.

"Do you need help?"

"I need to rest," the Man said. "Then you can tell me where I might find lodging."

He was either Snatch or the dumbest sailor I'd ever seen. Lodgings? In Five Points?

"Try Pete Williams' dive," I snapped, stepping forward, shielding David. "It's called Almacks and it's on Orange Street."[3]

"How do I get there?"

"I'll point the way," I said, for some reason less afraid than before.

"What ship you off, Mister?" It was David again.

The sailor coughed and stuttered. "The S.S. Jerry Mullens!"

"Never heard of that ship," David went on, "and you don't look like a sailor to me!"

He looked like one to me. He was twenty-four or so, rucksack over his shoulder, bandana tied around his

3

neck—yet frankly, I half-expected in the next second, to hear Snatch's terrifying whistle, feel the slimy burlap sack pulled over my head and find David and me the following morning chained in a boat headed south. I coulda' punched David! Surprisingly, the man just trembled—in fact he was trembling more than I was!

"I'm not a sailor," he said.

"What are you?" David continued.

"A cook's mate!"

David looked at me with his, *I-don't-believe-him* expression. For my part, I didn't care what the man was.

"It's getting dark, David," I said.

"When you get to Orange Street, you'd better watch your money!" David informed him.

"Oh, I only have a few coppers," said the man.

"One penny is a lot in some places in Five Points," I added.

"Is that where I am—Five Points?"

"Yep," I nodded. "And we better get going."

Am I soft-hearted? Not normally, but maybe it was the way he was trembling in front of two scrawny kids like us. We got our poles. David grabbed his bluegill and I hitched the bag to my belt. The cook's mate stood up slowly. He was a lot taller than I thought—and muscular.

"What's your name?" David again.

"Johnson—Freddie Johnson—what's yours?"

We told him. I knew Freddie Johnson wasn't his real name though. He hadn't said it with any confidence—like he had been using it all his life.

"I really appreciate the help," he said. "What's that on the bag?"

I told him what I thought it was, and if he saw that smiling skull again—anywhere, to leave where he was at once. David winked at me, and we started toward home and Pete Williams' gin mill.

"Thanks again. I'll repay you both, I promise."

Yeah, I thought. *This is the last we'll see of you!*

It didn't take us long to reach Leonard Street—a block away from home and Pete Williams' place.

"Which way is it?"

David pointed. I told him to turn right at the next corner, and Freddie started away. He wasn't half-way down the block when David whispered, "Let's follow him."

"Why?"

"I think he's a fugitive slave!"

"So what? I know he is!"

"How do you know?"

"Freddie Johnson's not his real name," I said, "and who else goes around changing their names but fugitives?"

"Let's follow him then—just suppose he gets into trouble?"

"So? What can *we* do?"

David shrugged. "Don't know. Daddy said, *whenever or wherever you can, help a fugitive*, remember?"

I remembered, dog-gone-it! I wanted to pop him one, though. David started behind Freddie forgetting his bluegill and pole, so I grabbed them—and yep, I followed too. I guess I might as well tell you, David's the brave one. Me? You guessed it—scared to death!

■ ■ ■

Sometimes a tale is as close to the truth as you can get. There is no way I can prove that what I'm about to tell you actually happened September 4th, 5th and during the weeks before my birthday. Largely, because the people who were involved in the events I'm about to reveal vowed never to tell anyone, for fear of getting their friends in trouble with the laws of New York State. 'Course, you can go to the *New York Times,* or *The Sun* to find the name of this or that person connected with these goings on, just to confirm they really existed, and that I'm not lying about a particular saloon or street. You can prove David and me are real, 'cause our father Robert Little, a member of the New York Committee of Vigilance, wrote his name at the bottom of a secret list of *conductors* on the Underground Railroad in 1837, adding our mother, Alice, and our names as next of kin. That is, if you can find that secret list. But even having done all that, none of the aforementioned suggestions would list the events as they happened or provide you with a clear picture! So, I guess you'll have to take my word for what I'm about to tell you.

David and me live in Five Points—a part of lower Manhattan. I have never been able to figure out why people continue to call it that—even though I know five streets—Cross Street, Anthony Street, Orange Street, Mulberry Street and Little Water Street intersect in the center of the neighborhood. It seemed to me that Five Points should have something to do with stars, night skies, and peace. Our mother told us that before she was born, the neighborhood was once the hub of aristocratic New York where a lake called the Collect was a place people came to picnic or fish.[4]

I don't mind saying, it takes a lot of imagination to see our streets flooded with ladies in carriages or gentlemen gallantly removing their capes so ladies can sit down and picnic. Five Points is said to be one of the worst slums in the United States! Savage! Violent! Bloody! And, if you don't believe it, the New York newspapers dare you to come down here at night *by yourself* and get back to wherever you came from, without scratch or broken limb!

You see, Five Points is *the* principal stop on the Underground Railroad in New York. I guess people who know that and think slavery's right, would naturally say this part of town is bad—what with all them fugitive slaves and free black men runnin' around. 'Course they're not entirely wrong! I've seen women fights, knife fights and dog fights! Seen a nameless fugitive chased by slave catchers until the pathetic man's legs gave way and sent him tumbling toward my Dad who, unable to help, watched silently as the Watchmen dragged him off.[5]

One night last winter, the wind blowing off the Hudson was so cold, it didn't even seem like wind. It felt more like chunks of a gale you could grab and

throw in wide, howling pieces, if you didn't freeze in
the process. I had crawled out of bed, real quiet-like,
in the deepest part of night, tip-toeing to the window,
trying not to make a sound. When I raised the canvas
to peep out on the alley below and Little Water Street—
you guessed it—David shoved his elbow into my side
so hard I nearly shouted.

"What you lookin' at, Charlie?"

"What are you doin' out of bed, David?"

"You woke me up!"

"I did n—!"

I saw them in that instant. A group of huddled black
figures inching their way along the sidewalk until they
reached a door. It opened suddenly. Swallowed them
instantly. Then slammed shut so quickly I wasn't sure
I'd even seen them. Several minutes after, the clatter
of horses enlivened the street. Our mother came into
the room while the Sheriff, two or three Watchmen
and four slave catchers rode up and down Little Water
Street, yelling about fugitive slaves, banging on doors
and waking people up. My dad, David and me were
born free black men. Our mother had been a slave
in Delaware, and a fugitive in New York. Whenever
we were careless, she'd sit us down and tell us about
slavery and what her life was like before she married
Dad. But that's another story, and I don't wanna tell
somethin' else—this tale is gruesome enough! Anyhow,
we live half-way up Little Water Street at #19, on the
second floor in two rooms. The Irishmen call our section *Staggtown*.[6] They live all around us on Anthony,

Mulberry, Leonard, Cross and Orange Streets. Now on parts of Cross Street, near Pearl and Centre Street—the people seem to be from everywhere else in Europe and speak strange languages and wear strange clothes. About the only thing people in Five Points have in common is poverty. My dad says: "Charles, when you git this many poor people togetha' nature just *makes* a slum, like the puddles after rain—wouldn't matta' where you dropped 'em!" Dad is something of a sage, I guess. But there aren't many situations in Five Points nowadays that call for a sage, so he's a chimney sweep.[7]

At times, durin' the summer, when he has lots of work, David and me—we'll go up to the Bowery and watch him climb three, maybe four stories into the sky! I'm going to start this story in a second—just want you to feel like you're here in Five Points with me.

Now, if you walk south down Little Water Street, you'll come to Paradise Square. My bet is, you'd smell it, long before you get there! I use'ta tell David it had the stink of dead rats mixed with the aroma of strawberries. It isn't really a square at all—more like a loose triangle, surrounded on all sides by dark, worn-out buildings that jut into the gray cobblestone streets. Most of them were old warehouses or sheds. Now, people live in them—or I should say *try* to live in them. Inside, the warehouses are so crowded, tenants build scaffolds and lay wooden planks every eight feet, living on top of each other in tiny personal spaces, each guarded, on every level by angry barking dogs—dogs, brought into a tenants layer and never allowed to leave. Oh, some folks walk them outside once a day, but most of those *growlers* never see much daylight. The warehouses are mazes of wood, hidden passageways and secret doors! Never walk beside them either! They say the safest place in Five Points is in the middle of the street! Whenever you look up, the few windows are stuffed with evil, bawling hags who'll dump garbage on your head and cackle afterward like green witches—or if it's nighttime, they might drop a noose around the neck of some unsuspecting passer-by and strip him of his money before letting the poor man go. Shucks—one morning on our way to school, David and I saw some unfortunate soul, barely breathing, rope still around his neck, stuffed beside the clapboard and wooden walls of a warehouse. And don't think it just happens to men!

In some of the sheds tenants raise pigs. You heard me correctly. I said pigs! Big grunting porkers with squealing piglets out at night hunting scraps of vegetables and food tossed onto the streets the day before. Eating all they can, then *beefing* back to their piggeries by dawn, half-stuffed, and leaving behind them a disgusting trail of offal that you dare not step in.[8] Makes me sick just to think about it. Give me a few minutes to let my stomach settle.

Remember I said you could smell Paradise Square? Well, you can hear it too!

"HOT CORN! HOT CORN!" "STRAWWWW-BERRRRIEEEEES!"

On mild days—like right now, before it gets cold, Paradise Square is flooded with street peddlers and hot corn girls. They come from every country, dressed in everything from drum major costumes to gaudy rags folded and wrapped around their bodies. The hawkers sell everything you could want. Corn to copper pots! Forks to flowers! Books to bludgeons!

"HOT CORN! Here's your nice hot corn—smoking hot, smoking hot, just from the pot!"[9]

■ ■ ■

I said I was gonna begin this story didn't I? Well, it started on the first day after nearly a week of rain—a day David and me decided to go fishin'. What I didn't tell you was, since Five Points is near the bottom of Manhattan, three sides of it are surrounded by water. On the east is the East River, south the ocean, on the west, the Hudson River. Ships moving in all directions. The day was cloudy—I remember that. David and me took our poles and headed for the Hudson River where we figured we'd hook a couple striped bass for dinner.

"I want you back before dark, Charles." Mother was standing in the doorway.

"I'll bring him back!" David said snickering.

Mother didn't have to worry about me. The day before, I overheard my father and Mr. Ruggles discussing a list of freemen shanghaied or kidnapped into slavery, and how the Black-Birders and Snatch had increased their activities.

I know, I know! I haven't mentioned the Black-Birders before. You see, Five Points is divided. On the north, above Paradise Square and the Old Brewery, the territory up to the Bowery is lorded over by a huge Irish gang called the Dead Rabbits, who we freemen call, Black-Birders, because their principal occupation—besides putting out fires and fighting—is snatching fugitive slaves and freemen off the streets and selling them into slavery. On the south, where we live, the area is bossed by the Roach Guards another gang of firemen, who spend most of their time fighting the Black-Birders and robbing sailors. Every now and then, they might kidnap a black man, but the Roach Guards hate the Black-Birders so much, whenever they see a black man in the clutches of a *Birder,* they free him out of spite and end up protectin' us! They don't want to, but that's how it's turned out. Now, the Committee of Vigilance has a lot of strong men in it too—and a Roach Guard or Black-Birder would take their lives into their own hands if they came looking for trouble on Little Water Street without the protection of a mob.[10]

It was September 4th—twenty days, fourteen hours until my birthday. I'd been counting off the time. Glad we didn't have to pass through Paradise Square, we left our house, headed over Anthony to Centre Street, up Centre to Lispenard, then west on Lispenard Street to the docks. David wanted to race.

"Last one to the docks is a dead rabbit!"

"No running—you heard Mom! If somebody sees us runnin' they're sure to think we're runaways and chase us, then where would we be?" Besides, we were on Lispenard Street where Mr. Ruggles, head of the Committee of Vigilance, lived. If he saw us fooling around he was sure to tell our parents, and I didn't need the tongue-lashing or punishment that would come out of that! David grunted. He always grunted when he was mad.

"I ain't scared, Charlie!"

"I am!"

'Course he grunted again and slowed down. By the time we got to the docks he was walkin' slower than a crawl. If there's one thing I've learned about David, it's to leave him alone when he's angry. We sat down on the edge of the docks. For a long time, he didn't say anything except, "Give me a worm!"

I gave it to him. He cast his line into the water. I threw mine in after his and waited.

There's nothing prettier in this world than the Hudson River. See, the Hudson's a blue river—I swear!—just a few shades darker than the sky, and even in winter when its half frozen over, it seems warm to me. Looking at it from Manhattan, you can see the shadow of the Palisades stretch beside it like a long, flat hat. It's some river all right—filled with ships, sailors—and pirates! Yep! In some of the coves near Croton are cutthroats worse than the Black-Birders. This day, the river was peaceful and quiet.

David got the first bite. Whatever kind of fish it was, that baby was tugging furiously on his line.

"I can do it! I don't need any help!"

Isn't that like a little brother? He's nearly falling off the dock and won't ask for help! I let him struggle with it for awhile, then stepped in, just as he was about to tumble into the Hudson.

"I won't fall!"

I didn't even answer—sometimes David can be a pain!

"Hold onto it, Davy! Until you get that hook out' its mouth, don't let it go, Boy!"

David and I turned around. Moving slowly toward us on a bright red, horse-drawn wagon loaded with kegs of beer was 'Smoke' Newsom. He was sitting on top of the kegs reining in the horses with one hand and waving his wide-brimmed, green felt hat with the other.

"How's the catch, Boys?"

"Just bluegill," David shrugged, holding up his catch, wriggling on the hook.

Now there are some things in this world that defy description—the feeling of family around you on holidays—whatever it is I notice, passes between my father and mother when they look at each other—both hard to describe! Yet, you only need one word to describe Smoke: BIG! Smoke Newsom is the biggest black man I've ever seen! He's not fat either! Smoke's got muscles he's never even used! He's about six and a half feet tall and the bouncer at Terry Logan's Fox Terrier Tavern. Smoke says he was a fugitive slave. He even boasted to David and me, how he broke his owner's back, then ran two weeks without stopping. Said he dove into the ocean and swam to New York, and once he got here, had the longest fight in Five Points history with Cow-Leg Tom McCarthy and his lady-friend Sadie, who would soon become Sadie-the-Goat, a river pirate. It took three weeks to beat them both and become the champion of

Five Points. *Everybody* but David is afraid of him—I am—that goes without saying! They say, even Snatch is afraid of Smoke! Every now and then somebody would try to shanghai Smoke, but the next day, you'd hear about two or three dead men found mysteriously floating in the East or Hudson Rivers.

"Tried to kidnap Smoke!" somebody would say.

"It ain't worth the money!" would be the reply—and believe me, it wasn't!

David put the squirming fish into our pail and Smoke laughed.

"That's kinda' big fish for a little guy like you Davy!"

"I ain't little," David shouted.

"You gonna be big as me soon!" Smoke shook his head, slapped the reins against the horse's rear and the wagon started to move.

"Be careful now—Snatch's on the prowl! Slavers are preparin' a big sale for Alabama—they gotta find more than fifty or sixty fugitives—or kidnap freemen to make up the total!"

Smoke waved as the wagon rolled away. I waved, then wished some unearthly power would prevent the wagon from leaving, for I had a feeling, I can easily describe as the creeps!

Now, I have talked about everything except Snatch. Only because I don't know—or let's say, *I didn't know* much about him at the time. Rumors said—and only in a whisper—that he was a slave, or former slave, who spent much of his time—for a price—helping Southern slave catchers find runaway slaves and transport them back into slavery. And when the quota of slaves was short of the desired number of runaways, Snatch would lure freemen or their woman and children into the slave catchers' clutches. There are people in this world so low-down, I can't imagine a word, rotten enough to call them—that's Snatch. He dresses up in disguises, acting friendly, until the unwary fugitive lets his guard down. Then Snatch blows on his whistle—a signal for his cut-throat friends to bum-rush the poor devil, toss a burlap hood over his head, shackle or tie him up, then carry him to the first boat heading south. The *very day* David and me went fishing, someone told our mother the two Cullen children, Mattie and Buster, had disappeared three nights before—frightening enough, except their house was locked from the inside, and no one broke in! Some of our friends swear Snatch can crawl under doors and floor boards. He's certainly low enough!

David and me looked at his catch. It was about the biggest bluegill I'd ever seen—maybe eight inches! David pointed at it frowning.

"I wanted a catfish!"

"Bluegill's taste better than catfish," I said. "Sweeter!"

"I don't care about sweeter—I wanted a catfish!"

I didn't feel like arguin'. I just shrugged and glanced down at my line. And here is where I began this tale.

My float was bobbing up and down in the Hudson River like something was trying to pull it under. Now that I think about the bag I hooked, and the skull drawn on it, I realize the belt inside it and the note belonged to Buster or Mattie Cullen. I hoped they escaped.

CHAPTER TWO

ONCE ON A DARE, I jumped into the Hudson River with all my clothes on—*in the winter time!* Yet, the most boneheaded thing I've ever done was telling that poor cook's mate, Freddie Johnson, to look for lodgings in Pete Williams' Almacks on Orange Street. One of the most notorious streets in Five Points, Orange Street slashes through the neighborhood heading south, where it dead-ends at Chatham Street, the boundary of the Sixth Ward. The street is so dangerous that the corner where Pete Williams' saloon is located is called Pint-A-Blood Point.[1]

I can remember overhearing Mr. Ruggles say to my father, "Robert, if you haven't murdered at least two or three people, you don't even qualify to walk from one end of Orange Street to the other!" As frightened as I was, I felt ashamed. I had blurted out, "Try Pete Williams' dive," without any concern for the consequences. What if something terrible did happen to

Freddie Johnson? It would be my fault for telling him to go to Pete's. I wanted to kick myself—or David. After all, he was the one who had gotten us both into this mess.

Cautiously, we followed Freddie. Walking a few steps, then crouching, in an effort not to be seen, I tried to slow David down.

"You want him to see us?"

"I don't want to lose him, Charlie!" David was whispering now—and practically tip-toeing down the street. Frankly, I thought we both looked pretty stupid.

"We won't lose him!"

We slowed to a stroll, as Freddie abruptly turned the corner and entered Orange Street.

Now, if you were the two of us, wouldn't it occur to you, that Freddie might be leading us into a trap? It occurred to me, as David and I approached the corner.

"Just suppose," I said to David, "this is some—some plan, to lure me and you into Orange Street, where this so-called Freddie—*who we really don't know*—who could be Snatch, is waiting on us with two heavy burlap sacks, ready to drop on both our heads as we turn the corner? *Annd,* just suppose we get sold into slavery. You and me are separated, forced onto different plantations, where slave drivers use wet, cowhide whips to make us work in the cotton fields, from sun up to sun down, and we both grow old and crotchety before we see each other again, and when we do, we don't recognize each other as brothers anymore—just *suppose* David! Dad would give us the beating of our lives—you know that?"

David grunted like he always does and continued to follow Freddie.

"Just *suppose* David."

"Awww, Charlie, c'mon!" he complained.

"C'mon where?" I stopped.

"Onto Orange Street!"

What made me mad was, I couldn't leave him! Our dad would've tanned me good if I came home without David. Had I grabbed him, and dragged him down the street, the ruckus he would have caused would've given us away. So, I followed, promising myself I would bop David a few times when we got home. The pleasure of knowing I'd pay him back for his stubbornness made me move faster.

We could hear the muffled shouting, and raucous noise mixed with music coming from Almacks before we turned the corner. The saloon is a low-slung white, wooden building, with a free-swinging sign that somebody painted a smiling, wide-eyed black devil on. The place is owned by a former black crook named Pete Williams—yep, I said crook! My father said Pete, a former slave (nobody could figure out how he got free) led a gang of thugs who preyed on crews and river boats that docked on the Hudson side of Five Points. Pete's reputation for clobbering men over the head had earned him the nickname, Pete the Brickbat. Many a sailor landed in the hospital, or was tossed in the river, a victim of Pete's gang—'course now, they say, Pete's retired. I'd never seen it, but my dad said, Pete had taken up singing—and *concert music!*

On Friday evenings, Pete would hold singing and dancing contests at the Almacks—contests he'd always enter—and usually lose. What I liked most about Pete though, were his get-ups! Pete wore the fanciest clothes in Five Points—ruffled collars, long coats, boots—and a bowler hat he never took off his head. It was rumored Pete hid a derringer pistol under it. No one alive could prove it. It was enough most people believed he had it, and like Smoke, most of them left Pete alone.

Just as we turned the corner, Freddie reached the doors. Out flies a drunken sailor, who stumbles a few steps, and before he can recover is jumped on by two of Pete's waitresses—Hammer Shanahan and Black Beeny Dobbs. David and me were too far from the saloon to hear or see it all, but Freddie told us later:

"I followed your directions and entered, what I don't mind telling you, was the seamiest alley I'd ever seen, and proceeded rather cautiously down its length to the corner, where Almacks stood, belching its rowdiness into the street like a fire-breathing reptile! As I approached the doors, a man—or what I assumed to be a man—was hurled into the street and attacked immediately by two women—or what I thought were women—followed by a sizable crowd that filled the doorway laughing and egging the ladies on!"

"Hit him one for me, Beeny!" David and me heard a dockhand yelling.

"Kick him good, Hammer!"

"Tear the clothes off that piker!"

"Of course, the two women took the advice of the hooligans and thugs seriously and laid into the poor devil, too drunk to defend himself. Hammer—I believe that was her name—kicked the man around the shoulders and arms, while Beeny beat him with her shoe. When the horrible deed was concluded and the man lay unconscious in the middle of the cobblestone alley, Hammer, who had charged after him cursing and smoking a cigar, dug into his pockets, removed his cash and started back into Almacks. The crowd was applauding and shouting.

"That'll teach that rat to make sure he gives me a tip for my services," Hammer boasted.

"Hold it, gip!"² It was Beeny. "Half that money belongs to me!"

Hammer turned toward this Beeny person slowly. "I rolled him—you just try and take it!"

Well, before Hammer could say another word, Beeny leaped on her and the two ladies began fighting each other. This time, they carried the fight into the saloon. For myself, I wasn't sure what to do. At first, I thought, Freddie, leave this place as fast as you can!

But two things tugged at me. First, I had no place else to go and second, what would happen if you two children had actually figured out I was a fugitive slave and had gone off to report me to the authorities? I made a choice quickly, following the crowd, unnoticed, back into the saloon. I couldn't see at first. The inside of Almacks wasn't lit well, and I stumbled as I crossed the threshold. Before I fell, I was snatched by the back of my collar and jerked upright into a corner beside one of the doors.

"Pay up, Mister!" The voice was low, gravelly. "Costs a penny to git in hea'!"

Fearful, I turned around. What I was confronted with was startling. It—or she—was a huge black woman—she must have weighed at least 350 pounds— sitting on an enormous stool, smoking a corn cob pipe. I was later to find out she was named Big Sue, but was known to most of the people in Five Points as The Turtle. She was also Pete's bouncer. She leaned back—a feat of no small accomplishment—eyed me curiously, turned her fat face down in an expression of disdain and snapped her fingers.[3]

"Pay up or git knocked down."

Without hesitating I dug into my pocket, removed a copper and gave it to her. Casually, she tucked it into her bosom, then nodded her head. I was too afraid to move.

"Git in, yah bum!"

Believe me, I hopped to it!"

Once Freddie walked into Almacks, it seemed to me, our job was done—after all, didn't we *follow* him? Wasn't that what we *agreed* to do? Before I could say, "Let's go home," David dashes into Orange Street, leaps over the poor fellow laying in the street and cautiously—as if he was a spy or something—creeps up to the doors of Almacks and along the side wall to a cluster of empty kegs beneath a window.

"DAVID!" I shouted, though it spilled out in a whisper.

I was really mad! I started after him, with the sole intention of breaking him in two or cracking his skull! It was one thing to put himself in jeopardy, but to unthinkingly disregard the danger his behavior could mean for others in times like these, when slave catchers roamed the streets of New York like bands of bloodsucking insects, was a crime. I moved just as the man Beeny and Hammer had beaten tried to stand! I was scared. I didn't know whether to stop or run! Should I go back? Leap over him? With two poles and a bucket of fish? He began to turn in my direction, and the glimpse I caught of this fellow's face told me, *Charlie, don't let him see you!*

"Jump him, Charlie!" David shouted. "Jump him!"

So, I jumped over him, crashing onto the cobblestones, tripping, nearly losing the bluegill, then scurrying to a place beside David, and behind three empty kegs. The man *hadn't noticed!* Still drunk, he rose slowly, tried brushing off his clothing, staggered a few steps toward Almacks and was broadsided in the face and knocked down again, when two men left the saloon and the opening door struck him. Poor devil! He really got his that day! The two men, both dockhands, laughed, lifted him—one under each arm—and dragged him unconscious to the corner, where they deposited him quietly, and rather neatly, beside Pete's flag pole, his hat in his hand.

The dockhands ambled away from Orange Street telling one another vulgar jokes, yet cackling like embarrassed hens. David climbed onto the empty kegs and tried to peep into the window of Almacks, but he was too short. When he asked me to look, I refused.

"That's not fair, Charlie!"

Fair? Didn't he have a nerve? I decided to ignore his remark. I turned in the direction of Little Water Street, imagining our mother standing at the door.

"It's getting dark, and we're supposed to be home!"

"I'm not goin', until you climb up!" David crossed his arms over his chest.

"I'm not climbing!"

"Then I'm not going!"

There is no need to repeat that dumb conversation! David is the most stubborn, muleheaded, lockjawed—anyway, while my brother and me—and I use the word *brother* lightly—while David and me stood outside arguing, Freddie moved into the heart of the saloon. After what he told us, I'm glad I wasn't him!

"Gradually my eyes grew accustomed to the light in Almacks. What I saw terrified me! The saloon was no more than a large white-washed, I-shaped room, with a long bar on the left, and a small platform behind it. The floor was covered with sawdust. In the center of the place an empty area to dance was outlined by a half-circle of small tables where some men gambled, while others watched. My description seems mild—almost tame, doesn't it? However, filling every inch of space so described, were the most notorious, ragged, dangerous

bunch of swamp and river rats my eyes had ever seen! And I had spent a considerable part of my life around boats and seamen, witnessed horrors that branded my soul, yet I had never observed in one place, at the same time, the likes of these people—and I shudder at the use of that word to describe human beings who seemed so entirely divorced from any semblance of humanity! Lord save us! Every size, color and description of men and women were there. Some men, sailors and deck-hands, stood at the bar drinking whiskey from hose[4] or bottle and thumping one another on the shoulders, in gestures that I've been told were friendly, but certainly would have broken my back! Other men were dancing jigs or jubas—while still others sat at tables drinking from tankards of beer and rum. Yet, if it is conceivable to think this motley rabble gentle, by comparison the women in this place made these men seem like gentle sheep slumbering in the greenest of pastures. They completely defied description. There was not so much as a single distinguishable face among them, so covered with paint and rouge were they. These women were of every race—black, white, some Indian, and I believe I noticed two or three Chinese—it barely seemed to matter what they were, so struck were my eyes by their outfits and their outrageous behavior. I recall think-ing—perhaps my only pleasant thought—that 'the color of their clothes mirrored the rainbow.' But when a tankard sailed past my head, and the woman who threw it shouted a string of obscenities at the drunken sea captain scurrying to get out of her way, my mind went back to the terrifying scene before me. Some of the women flirted with men at the bar, others cuddled up with men at tables. Still others hugged in corners or wrestled over the few pennies flung at them by the most hideous of men, who seemed to enjoy watching the women cut and scratch each other for their meager rewards. Indeed, the fight between Beeny and Hammer still went on in the middle of the place and though a small crowd had gathered, the majority of this group paid little or no attention to it. And lest I be accused of singling out the women—in truth, everyone in this den maintained full equality with everyone else. I was certain there wasn't an honest person among them, and very cautiously I inched my way in the direction of Pete Williams. I am not sure how I knew the man I moved toward was Pete Williams except to say of all the men in this unholy room, he was the only person who seemed above everything around him, and, I might add, the only person everyone took care not to bump into or annoy.

He stood beside the bar, his elbow leaning casually on it, occasionally barking orders to several women who moved about, quickly filling tankards with beer and whiskey. His black bowler hat seemed glued to his head. As I moved toward him, I wondered what could possess this diminutive man to operate such a place. Certainly his own morals must have been as low as those of the people who made this place their unholy stomping ground! I didn't get far, however. Suddenly a man, whom I would later find out was *called Pickles the Killer, leaped onto the bar beside Pete. Unquestionably one of the foulest-looking denizens in Almacks, his shoulder-length hair hung down in ringlets around his pock-marked, unshaven face, and even from where I was standing, the odor of the man rose with him and fanned out in all directions, as if a stench had been introduced unknowingly into the room. But more gruesome than his own appearance were the two huge rats Pickles held, one in each hand. Through blue, bloodshot eyes he stared at them greedily. He shouted something unintelligible, and suddenly bit off both rats' heads, and threw their squirming bodies onto Hammer and Beeny! The heads he tossed into the crowd watching the women. It goes without saying that the two women stopped fighting and let out screams that could have awakened the dead—and all of this was watched with amusement and downright gaiety by the crowd and Pete Williams. The person laughing the loudest was Pete! He nearly collapsed at the base of the bar. Pickles, blood spilling from his lips, spit onto the floor, rinsed his mouth with beer and joined the frivolity. I had thought to leave the place then, but the crowd had filled in the space behind me, and all I was left to do was press ahead to Pete, a man who I no longer wanted to meet. As I moved, Beeny shot past me screaming frantically and wiping the rat blood from her shoulders, neck and back. It was at this point that I felt myself grow dizzy. Perhaps it was the smoke—the stench—I am not sure, but suddenly the room tilted—began to sway. I made one last effort to reach the bar, practically throwing myself in its direction. I was more than surprised when I felt its wooden security against my stomach holding me up. I am not sure how long I stood there. Seemed like hours. When my head began to clear, I straightened. The time had apparently been no more than momentary, since Pete who stood beside me was still laughing at Hammer, who had begun to scream and throw whatever she could grab at Pickles who dodged and laughed. I turned to Pete, and surely made the biggest mistake of my life. I spoke.*

"Excuse me, Sir," I said, "if you are Pete Williams, I have been told you might provide me with lodgings for the night."

The man never stopped laughing. Instead of answering me, he grabbed my arm and flung me with tremendous force, away from the bar and back into the crowd, where I collided with several men and fell onto the floor.

"Hey! We've got us a dancer!" he yelled. "Show him how we dance in Almacks!"

My sack was snatched from me and I was lifted bodily from the floor and almost tossed into the center of the dance floor, where I was then pushed and shoved from person to person until I fell again, nearly unconscious. For some reason, I remember telling myself to stand up—and so I tried, but without the desired results. Each time I would try, someone or something would push me back onto the sawdust-covered floor. It was only when a woman poured beer on my head, that in sheer anger I stood and began fighting back with no success. What seemed like a giant lifted me and tossed me across several tables—and I don't mind telling you, I thought as I flew through the air—this is the end! I crashed into a chair and realized I would not be able to rise this time. This time I was beaten, and from the corner of my eye, I caught the hulking image of this massive giant who had tossed me, moving in, fuming, growling, prepared to make the final kill. I was sure to die."

■ ■ ■

"I'm not goin'!"

Would you believe David and me were still arguin'? There are some things just too silly to believe, and our argument was one of them! Here we were, in the worst part of Five Points arguin' over something dumb—something so stupid—well, I decided it wasn' worth it anymore and rather than continue it, I started to walk away.

"Wait Charlie!"

"I'm goin' home," I said.

"Don't you want to see what happens to him?"

"No!"

"Awwww—" David reluctantly followed me a few steps. I'll say this, as we headed away, I was relieved! What surprised me though was why I hadn' done this before? 'Course, David was grunting again, and walkin' as slow as a turtle, but I didn't care—all I wanted to do was get home—but it was not to be—nope!

29

Without warning, Blind Elias the Frog, an old man who had gained his reputation around Five Points pretending to be blind and collecting huge sums of money beggin' north of the Bowery, charged onto Orange Street yellin' at the top of his voice.

"Git off the streets! Git off the streets! The Roachies and Black-Birders are havin' it out tonight in Paradise Square! Git off the streets!"

This was the first time I can recall David and me being terrified in unison. God Almighty! When the Roach Guards and the Black-Birders fought in Paradise Square, it was unsafe for blacks—free or fugitive—to be on the streets. Our dad said the disputes went back as far as he could remember—when the Irish first began to settle in Five Points. Seems like, at one time, the Black-Birders use'ta be part of the Roach Guards, and had split off over somethin' pretty small—by now, it didn' seem to matter, and the reason probably had been lost long before I was born. Anyway, whateva' the reason, the worst sight in Five Points was to see the Roach Guards in their blue-striped pantaloons, undershirts and plug hats, confront the Black-Birders in their red-striped pants, undershirts and bowlers.[5]

I swear, such a mess of knives, bludgeons, brickbats, blackjacks, pistols and paving stones, you ain't neva' seen! Blind Elias the Frog's shouting was like a signal. For me it spelled—R-U-N! But not for David—he wanted to help Freddie!

"Freddie who?"

"C'mon, Charlie, we can't leave him—we sent him in there!"

He did have a point, but Freddie didn't have to go into Almacks—and what adult who isn't crazy actually listens to two kids? *No,* I thought, *Freddie is gonna git himself outta this one!* I started away.

"Please, Charlie?"

Now there are some things that are rare—so rare that you not only don't see them, you don't even hear about them—and the only people that know about them lived way back in history like the Romans, and they only half-mumbled something about these rare things, and were almost overheard by a passerby who was deaf in one ear! A *please* from David is one of those things. Once heard, the sound has to be preserved in the memory for all time—since it is highly unlikely that it will ever be heard again! 'Course I agreed to help—not just because of that, but Blind Elias the Frog's shouting had started a stampede out of Almacks and David was right in its path! I ran back, snatching his arm, and pulled him to one side of the door, where behind the empty kegs, we could wait out the on-rushing wave of men scurrying from the saloon. As we huddled in the corner, I wondered about Freddie and whether or not he had gotten a room.

Room? The huge thing coming at me might have had a permanent resting place in mind for me, but it certainly wasn't a room! I looked up and though he was at least six feet away I could feel his breath, imagined his fists beating me into a pool of blood and flesh. Then suddenly, as if the Lord Himself had stuck out His mighty hand, this bull—this giant called Dog-head Louis, stopped in his tracks, turned around, and with the others in this crowd, sprinted for the door! I didn't hear Blind Elias the Frog, until I was standing and dazed, gathering up my things and stuffing them in my sack. Who were the Roachies? The Black-Birders?

"Hey Sonny, don't git caught on the street!"

"Why?"

"Jest don't!"

Pete was moving to his windows, locking and shuttering them. Most of the women were going upstairs, and much to my surprise only Pete, Big Sue and myself seemed to be moving without haste. Big Sue moved laboriously toward the stairs, stopping only once to say to me in her gravel voice:

"Git out!"

I was not someone you had to tell twice! I grabbed my bag and headed for the door!

For awhile, as the men ran from Almacks, David and me thought the worst had happened to Freddie—after all, he wasn' among them, and the reputation of the saloon was enough to make me scared that someone had done him in! Luckily, he came out.

"Freddie!" David called after him.

Freddie stopped for a moment, saw the two of us, and shook his head.

"Did you get the room?"

"Did I? Look, I want to thank you two for helpin' me, but please don't give me anymore advice!"

"But you don't understand," David said, "the Black-Birders and the Roach Guards are getting ready to fight!"

"So?"

"You've got to get off the street!"

Frightened, Freddie turned around. Doors and windows were slamming shut on Orange Street.

"Where can I go?"

"With us!" David said.

"With us?"

David nodded.

"We can take him home, Charlie, if he don't git off the street they'll shanghai him!"

Before I could object, David was running down Orange Street, around the corner to Anthony Street, headed toward Little Water. And I bet you guessed it? Yep, me and Freddie followed—Freddie confused, me shouting at David, "Daddy don't allow us to bring no strangers home—you know that!" 'Course, I completely forgot the poles and David's bluegill.

But, by the time Freddie and I reached the corner, David was racing toward home—and none too soon—I could hear the yelling and shouting of the Roach Guards behind us. They were on their way to Paradise Square. Needless to say, Freddie and I ran so fast we nearly caught up with David, and I wish we had.

Chapter Three

H E WAS TWENTY RUNNING STEPS away from the intersection of Orange and Anthony Street when it happened. Like a huge cobra popping from a snake charmer's basket, Simon the Tease, sprang from the corner of the last building on Anthony Street and, unable to slow down, David ran into him. The collision nearly knocked the Tease off his feet, but the man was agile. A well-known panel thief,[1] shoplifter and pickpocket, noted for his uncanny ability to escape the clutches of some of the fastest-running Watchmen and cart owners in Five Points, the Tease caught himself before stumbling, and snatched his bludgeon from his rear pocket. Swinging it playfully, though with some menace several inches from David's head, he frightened him into stopping, and taunted him until David cried.

"Watch where you're running before I crown you one, you gutter rat," he snarled, baring a set of rotten teeth.

The Tease had been given his name because of his bullying. He was a tall, skinny, black man with the biggest feet and hands of anyone in the neighborhood. Wearing a wide-brimmed straw hat, preacher's coat, workman's boots and red-checkered scarf year round, combined with a voice that sounded like chalk scraping slate, the Tease was probably one of the strangest—and annoying—people in Five Points. But September the fourth was not one of the Tease's best days.

"Leave him alone!"

Freddie had raced past me and was, *that close* to the Tease.

"An' who de' hell might you be, Cousin?"

The Tease raised his bludgeon, but before he could swing it, Freddie snatched the club and struck the Tease once on his arm.

"Somebody who ain't lettin' you bully this boy, you grimy scarecrow!"

The blow was so painful, the Tease went down on one knee cursing and flailing his other arm at Freddie, who threw the bludgeon into the street, put his arm around David's shoulder and walked off toward Little Water Street. As I started up Anthony Street behind them, I realized Freddie had just given birth to a life-long enemy in the Tease. He called Freddie everything but a child of God, and threatened him as well.

"Don't let me see you agin fugitive—I know that's what you are, and there ain't no place in Five Points safe for a black runaway like you! You hea' me?"

A black woman shouting from a second floor window interrupted the Tease.

"Y'all betta' git off the streets—don't you see the Roachies comin'?"

The Tease glanced down the street behind us. A mob of Roach Guards were racing toward us and the Tease took off like a bullet. Didn't even look back to threaten again. He "just ran his butt off"—as my Dad would say.

I heard David tell Freddie something about Robber's Alley, but we had reached the house, and a turn of my key got us inside the front door just as the Roachies turned into Cross Street and Paradise Square. Whew! Safe at last!

■ ■ ■

"Where have you two been, and who are you, Mister?"

It was our dad, Robert Little, who is not *little* at all. He was standing at the head of the stairs on the second floor, just our side of the bannister, with his coat and hat on, fists on his waist, glaring at Freddie. The word *trouble* can't come close to describing what I knew David and me were in for. We both shuddered. Me? Most things scare me, but even David is scared of our dad—especially when he believes we've been careless about our safety.

"I've been worried out of my mind," our mother, Alice, said. She walked forward behind our dad with a look on her face that made me want to cry.

"You know the slave catchers stole the Cullen's, Mattie and Buster! How could you be so uncaring, Charles?"

Charles?

"You're the oldest and *I* rely on you to be the most level-headed!"

I won't say how I felt. I lowered my head so much I thought it would drop off my shoulders and roll down the stairs behind us. The two of them greeting us the way they did, only made matters seem worse.

Outside the door, the sound of the Roachies carousing down Little Water Street, drinking, cursing and threatening us and our neighbors, rose like the bellow of a giant whale beached on the banks of the Hudson River. We continued up slowly, but Dad stopped Freddie halfway up the stairs.

"I asked you who you were, *Mister*." There it was again, that booming voice that could frost the sun on the hottest day of summer. Dad took a few steps down the staircase, as he gestured David and me to pass him. There was a look of menace in his eyes.

"Ah—ah, Freddie Johnson, Sir," Freddie took a step backward, stammering.

"That's just a name!"

"Cook's mate off the S.S. Jerry Mullens, Sir!"

"What are you doing with my boys?"

"He stopped Simon the Tease from hitting me with his club, Daddy!" It was David.

Thank God for younger brothers!

"We were running home ahead of the Roach Guards, with the fish we caught," I added, "an'—an' the Tease jumped out and woulda' got us shanghaied if Mr. Johnson hadn't stepped in!"

Our dad softened somewhat, stretching out his hand to shake, just as Trimmer Spurts, our first floor neighbor, flung his door open, stuck his head out and shouted up to Dad.

"You hea' 'em Bobby? Is your boys safe?" Trimmer always called Dad, 'Bobby.' He was an injured ex-trapper and scout, who'd fought beside President Andrew Jackson in the War of 1812. He had a medal for bravery and though he worried David and me with his constant warnings about everything, from ghosts to rainbows, we always knew he had our best interests at heart.

"They're safe, Trimmer," Dad said.

"I seen 'em running with this fella here—yah did a good job on the Tease, fella—good job!" Having said that, Trimmer disappeared behind the door he slammed shut.

"I want to thank you for that, Mr. Johnson, but I'm afraid I'm going to ask you to leave."

"What about the Roachies," I asked rather timidly. *No reason to get my head chewed off for a fellow I still didn't know—or completely trust.*

"I wouldn't send a rat into a mêlée between the Roachies and the Black-Birders! Mr. Johnson, you can rest here for awhile, but as soon as the hot tempers cool down, you'll have to leave."

"Fair enough," Freddie replied.

"As for you two! Into your room! You're headed to *bed!* If you can't follow my instructions, maybe no dinner can teach you to listen!"

David started to speak, but Dad caught him before he could offer a protest.

"And not a word from either of you!" He pointed toward the rear of the second floor and we shuffled away quietly, waving a hand toward Freddie.

"Thanks, fellas," he said.

David was so upset he went straight to our bed, fell across it and cried. Me? I was as hungry as a bear waking from hibernation—and worried about Freddie.

■ ■ ■

"Your father was grateful for the help I gave, but he explained straight away: "I'd like nothing more than to offer you the hospitality of our home, Mr. Johnson. But circumstances here in New York—and especially in Five Points at this time—won't allow for any weakening of our vigilance against slave hunters. They have hired men of our own color for little more than pennies—men who seek out, and turn in innocent and runaway alike! My wife and I are grieving the loss of a neighbor's two children—both free—who were

kidnapped and sold to the South this past week. We think. I'm not accusing you of being such a person, Mr. Johnson, but I'm sure you can understand, until I know more about you and where you came from, I can take no chances!"

Sadly I agreed with him, having met an old friend of mine on the docks prior to meeting you two. He was so scared he didn't even want to speak to me. Indeed he asked me to walk behind him so no one would guess we knew one another. He had changed his name and told me: "Don't trust nobody! An' stay clear of de' churches and meetin' halls where we go, 'cause they're bein' watched by the New York Kidnapping Club!" Afraid to say anything else, he dashed into the street, dodging several carriages. He left me alone surrounded by freemen, yet afraid to speak to anybody.[†]

Once the disturbance seemed over, I shook your father's hand, thanked him and your mother for sheltering me from the mêlée of the Roachies and Black-Birders, and started out. Before I reached the door, I turned around remembering the name of the only person I was to meet once I arrived in New York.

"Pardon me, Mr. Little, but would you know of a colored gentleman called, David? I'm afraid that's all I know."

Your parents looked at one another furtively, then shook their heads 'no,' in a nearly comic unison with your father adding; "There are lots of Davids, Sir! Is that a family name?"

"I don't know. That was all I was told."

41

"We'd need to know more than that, Sir," your
mother reinforced.

The door was opened and I was back out on the
street trying to remember if you had said "Robert's Alley"
or "Robbers Alley." And where could it be, whatever
it was called?

When I heard the door open and close, I rushed
to the window. David had fallen asleep on the bed. I
watched Freddie walk toward Anthony Street quickly,
then stop near the end of the block and suddenly start
running.

Oh my God! What happened?

"I walked away from the house, with the words of
my friend and your father echoing in my head—"Don't
trust nobody!"—"I can take no chances!" Doors
and windows closed as I passed. It was the first time
I understood how dangerous life could be, even for
freemen, in the North. I had almost reached Anthony
Street when someone yelled.

"You a fugitive ain't yah?"

I looked up. Leaning from a second-story window
was an old, bespectacled black man, raging madly and
shaking his fists at me.

"I know you is! You from Saginaw, South Carolina,
ain't yah? I know your daddy an' your momma!"

He was shouting and calling attention to me. I started
walking faster, and before I left the block I was running.
Behind me I could hear the fading shouts and taunts
of the Roach Guards and Black-Birders too busy with

one another and too far away to pay attention to a lone
cook's mate. But closer to me I heard someone holler—
"Stop him! He's a fugitive!"
I raced toward the Hudson River. While I wasn't
sure what I'd encounter, having lived a good part of
my life around ships and men of the sea, I felt I would
be safer near the water than anywhere else. The streets
were still dangerous however, so I clung to the shadows
as I made my way toward the smell of the ocean and
the slap of the waves."

I heard someone climbing the stairs to the second
floor a few minutes after Freddie left. I wasn't sure who
it was, but it sounded like Mr. Ruggles, the head of the
New York Committee of Vigilance.[2] He lived north of
us on Lispenard Street.

"I saw him leave. Who was he Robert?"

I crept toward the slightly open door of our room
and laid on the floor listening.

"He stopped the Tease from annoying my David
before the mêlée. Said his name was Freddie Johnson,
cook's mate on the S.S. Mullens. He asked me if I knew
a man called David."

"Me?"

"Might have been, but we took no chances."

"There's word that a man is arriving from Maryland,
but the S.S. Mullens operates out of Savannah, Georgia!"

There was a knock at the door and when my father
opened it, the voice was clearly that of Mr. Bowman—
Ole'-Hit-You-With-A-Switch Moses Bowman, our
teacher in the Colored Free School near Five Points.[3]

"I saw him when he left, Robert," Ole'-Hit-You-With-A-Switch said. "He isn't a fugitive is he?"

"I don't know what he is, Moses. He helped my David, and I wouldn't have let the devil walk into a fight between the Roachies and the Black-Birds!"

"We have to be careful, Robert!"

"We all know that, Moses." My father sounded exasperated.

I imagined Ole'-Hit-You-With-A-Switch rubbing his hands together the way he did in school whenever he was excited. Right before he'd hit us.

"I can't afford to lose any more students, Robert! The loss of the two Cullen children endangered the school! The city may decide to close our school if we don't keep our enrollment up!"

"People come into New York every day, Moses," Mr. Ruggles said.

"Fugitives have no money for books—and—and school things, Ruggles! They can barely buy food! We have *got* to find this Snatch and expose him! He puts everything we try to do for freemen at risk! Everything! You think Snatch could be an ally of that fella who helped your David?"

"Unlikely," my father replied. "We lost neighbors long before this fella showed up."

"What was his name again?"

"He didn't offer it, and I didn't ask," father lied.

Wonder why?

Ole'-Hit-You-With-A-Switch didn't stay long after that. One moment his voice was there and the next it was gone.

"We have to find this Freddie Johnson for two reasons, Robert," Mr. Ruggles said. "Number one is, he may be the man I'm looking for from Maryland, and the second reason is, he could be connected to Snatch and if he is, he must be exposed!"

My father agreed. "Where do you think he'll go?"

"I don't know, but I'll pass his description on to the Vigilance Committee. We'll find him soon enough!"

"Who's Dad talking to, Charlie?" It was David. I told him, and he turned away and went back to bed. I moved back to the window. Outside, Little Water Street was deserted. I was still worried about Freddie but he told us later:

"When I stopped to catch my breath, I thought I was safe. The Hudson River was less than a hundred yards away, and I had climbed up a mountain of cargo stacked in large cases outside a waterfront warehouse, slid down into a narrow space between several cases, and was resting when I heard a dog growl. Couldn't tell what breed it was, but its snarl came from deep down in its throat and its eyes fixed me in a stare that dared me to move. I didn't. Instead, I froze where I was. The dog barked several times but didn't move. It seemed confounded—caught off balance, until suddenly it glanced upward and began to wag its tail and jump around in tight circles as some sort of food was dropped in its path.

"You're a lucky fella," the voice came from above, but I didn't dare move. "Ole' Dog has torn so many men your size to pieces, I started notching his collar! I guess you want to get out of there, huh?"

(I was to learn, as time passed, that New Yorkers in general had a talent for understatement.)

"Git away from him, Ole' Dog! Go 'head!"

Ole' Dog hesitated for a second.

"Now!" The voice was sharp and threatening. I almost felt sorry for Ole' Dog, but as I rose slowly, realizing the huge bullmastiff before me hadn't bit off my arm, I was profoundly grateful to whoever it was above me. When I looked up, the man's face was in the shadows.

"Name's Smoke Newsom," he said. As he moved he seemed the biggest man I'd ever seen. "I saw you with the boys and watched you protect 'em from the Tease, so I decided, when I saw you slide down in between these here cases, I wouldn' let Ole' Dog have your leg for dinner."

"Thanks!"

He reached down, offering his hand to grab, and lifted me upward in one quick pull. He was at least a foot taller than I, and his girth would have made one and a half of me. Yet he wasn't fat! I stood for several moments simply staring at him.

"I won't ask if you're a fugitive slave, but when you finish gaping at me, maybe you could tell me where you were headed?"

"One of the boys told me to look for either Robert's—or Robber's—Alley!"

"It's Robber's Alley—an' that ain't a safe place on a night when the Roachie and Black-Bird wounded will

be looking for poor black and Chinese men to retaliate against. You bes' follow me!"

I did, and the Five Points he led me through was more dangerous than Robber's Alley.

For a man his size, Smoke moved like an antelope. He was off the cases and on the ground outside the warehouse in seconds. I followed but just as I landed, we were greeted by the loud, drunken shouts of Black-Birders. A handful had been barfing into the Hudson River on the port side of the sloop, S.S. Peconic, a ship I'd seen off the coast of New Jersey before I landed in New York. Now they were pointing at Smoke and myself, cursing and calling us despicable names. Smoke laughed. He took a few steps forward into the street and yelled at them, cupping his hands over his mouth.

"You're a bunch of drunken Birdie bums! You hear me? You couldn't take down ole' ladies with canes or crutches!" Two or three of them broke into a run toward us screaming.

"You're dead, you piece of crap!"

"Dead," another yelled.

"Are you planning on fighting them," I asked. I didn't want to appear afraid, but there was a lump in my throat, growing larger at every step the Black-Birders took toward us. Behind the three that were charging forward, two others seemed to have regained a clearheadedness that now allowed them to start running at us as well.

"That's only Dicky the Map, and a few others. You're not afraid are you?"

"No!" I tried hard to sound confident, but at my best I didn't believe for a moment we could defeat five men! It was then Smoke bent over, lifted a circular piece of metal from the street and tossed it aside as if it were a scrap of paper.

"They won't follow us down there," he said gesturing toward the hole he'd just uncovered. I peeped. There was nothing in the hole but dark. "You game?"

"Do I have a choice?"

"None," he said, and dropped into the hole. Gone—and I did the only thing a sensible man could do, since the Birdies were eight feet away and prepared to leap at me. I dropped down the hole behind Smoke and landed on a pile of mattresses stuffed with hay. I had no sooner hit, than I was yanked up by Smoke.

"Pull the mats away from the hole," he bellowed.

I grabbed at the mattresses and tugged in the direction I felt Smoke pull, just as the first Birdie dropped down the hole after us and broke one of his legs on the cobblestones that lined the passageway beneath the warehouse. The poor man screamed his head off.

"What happened to yah, Donald?" His friends above had stopped and were peering down the hole, as Donald kept screaming.

"Get a torch!"

"Too bad boys!" Smoke shouted up at them laughing. "Better tell them, Dicky—never follow where you ain't never been!"

"You'd better not ever come up, you devil," one of the Birdies shouted from above.

"See you tomorrow," he shouted back.

They cursed us, but Smoke ignored them and pulled the mats farther away from the hole and the screaming Donald.

"Let's go," he said, moving off into another part of the passageway. By now my eyes were accustomed to the dark and I could follow his movements, the way one would trail a darker shadow in a starless night. "Dicky the Map knows these tunnels. Being down here is bad enough, but having them catch us would be undignified."

Undignified? In this underground world of foul smells and the din of rats? Amidst the wailing of the Birdie with the broken leg, I could hear a cacophony of squeals and screeches in every direction. Rats were living out their wretched lives all around me. Ahead of us were three passageways. Smoke headed toward the one on the left, which sloped downward about twenty feet, then veered sharply to the right and opened on a hub where four passageways presented themselves. He took the one farthest away on the right, where the rats seemed to be thickest, but once we were inside he stopped abruptly.

"Follow me across the shallow water ahead until we reach the mud," he said, "then grab my hand and step carefully until I stop again, then we'll back track in our own footsteps to the water again, where I'll lead you to the Old Brewery."

He explained that we were near what had been the Collect Pond which had been filled in years before.

The Tombs Prison was built above us, and though the builders had used hemlock trees to form its foundation, there were still tunnels where the underground stream that fed the pond still flowed and left passageways only a few knew about.

"Backtracking in our own footsteps will slow Dicky the Map down and guarantee his drunken Birdie bums will never find us," he laughed.

I tried to feel good about escaping the Birdies but the endless screeching and squeals of the rats left me nearly paralyzed with fear for my safety. I am not a man fearful of most things but the agitation of these creatures left me frightened for my life.

I trailed behind Smoke for at least another ten minutes when we came to a large circular wooden wall. Though it appeared seamless as we approached it, Smoke pressed against its left side and a door opened.

"Step into my parlor," he said, gesturing me in ahead of him. What I entered was a narrow wooden room that was obviously Smoke's home. "You can rest on the rug in the corner."

I was wet, exhausted and grateful. I said, 'Thank you,' laid down on the rug and fell asleep at once."

■ ■ ■

Mr. Ruggles left our parents not long after Ole'-Hit-You-With-A-Switch Bowman. Dad and Mother talked for awhile before he blew out the lantern in their room and got into bed. While David rested on the bed, he didn't sleep. When I moved back to the bed he said, "We didn't tell Dad about that bag you found with the skull on it, Charlie. I think those initials were Buster Cullen's." In the face of Dad's anger I had forgotten about the bag and what was in it.

"I'll tell him tomorrow," I said and tried to get comfortable in bed. I was tired and wanted to go to sleep.

"What if Freddie's hurt, Charlie?"

I opened my eyes and stared at the ceiling.

"I'm worried," I admitted. "But what can we do?"

"Something," David said. "I don't know what, but something."

I turned away from David, but it would be a long time before either of us went to sleep.

CHAPTER FOUR

W E BOTH SAT UP AT the same time. It was
nearly an hour before midnight and David
and me decided we'd never get to sleep if we didn't find
out what happened to Freddie.

"Where should we start looking?" I asked.

"Robbers Alley!"

"Shhh! Don't talk so loud!" I whispered, not want-
ing Dad to overhear us. Robbers Alley was bad enough
in the daylight. The idea of moving around it at night
didn't make me feel good about hunting for Freddie.
And what if he wasn't where we could find him? Night
brought slumming parties down to Five Points, uptown
groups in search of fun, cheap booze, loose women
and things David and me weren't permitted to talk
about. Children caught out at night were easy prey for
debauchers, shanghaiers and slave catchers. "What if
he's somewhere else?"

"Dirty Ida, will know."

"Dirty Ida? Don't make jokes, David!" Dirty Ida Washington was the prettiest, though toughest, foul mouthed girl in the Free Colored School. Along with her best friends, Two-tooth Clarabella Osbourn, and Irish Mabel Schultz, they formed The Brewery Witches, a loose group of girls who were crossing-sweepers, known to filch fruit and vegetables from Paradise Square carts and greengrocers, then disappear into the Old Brewery before anyone could catch them.[1] They were surprisingly good students though—Dirty Ida, despite her bad mouth (a condition my mother described as simply the sound of poverty), was the smartest girl in her class. Her friends went to the white Free School, where Two-tooth Clarabella was the best speller in her grade—and no one knew more about the Roachies and Black-Birders than Irish Mabel who wasn't Irish but German, and was thought to be Irish because she had flaming red hair and freckles.

"Dirty Ida knows every inch of Robbers Alley— annd, she likes you!"

I bopped him on that one.

"Stop it!"

"You want to wake Mom and Dad?"

"I will if you hit me again! Everybody knows she likes you!"

"Well, I don't like her," I said, but I had to admit, sadly, I didn't have a solution that would lead us to anyone else.

We dressed quietly. I don't think we were exactly sure why we wanted to find Freddie. I believe we both felt it was the right thing to do. After all, we had gotten him into whatever danger we thought he was in, and despite the risk to himself, Freddie had taken on the Tease, shepherded us to safety, and never asked for compensation.

Our bedroom had two windows. One looked out onto the back of the tenement we lived in. The other, onto the narrow alley between our place and #17, and Little Water Street. Reverend Eugene Caufield, a friend of Dad's, lived on the first floor next door. There were two drawbacks to leaving the house by the alley window though. The first, it was a window whose frame swelled after every heavy rain, which made opening it nearly impossible. The second, was a tin roof that slightly extended over the alley and made a lotta noise if you walked on it in shoes. So, we tied our shoes together and hung them around our necks. I grabbed a wad of wax from beneath a candle on our desk, then we tiptoed to the alley window, raised the canvas, turned up the latch—and waited. We didn't hear anything, or anyone, stirring. So, I took the wax and tried to force some of it between the frame and the window hoping it would help the window slide outward easily. It did, but I pushed too hard and the screeching noise the window made against the frame sounded loud enough to wake the dead!

"Everybody in the world could hear that, Charlie!"

"Get in bed without a sound," I whispered.

David and me jumped into bed, covered up, and pretended to sleep. The sound of Dad rising from his bed, crossing the squeaky boards from their room to ours was nearly immediate. My eyes closed a hairs-breath before he stuck his head into our room, peered around and whispered:

"Boys? You asleep?"

Thankfully neither David or me said "yes." Dad lingered for another moment or two, closed our door and went back to bed.

David wanted to get up at once, but I knew Dad would wait for awhile, listening for any noise that seemed out of the ordinary before going back to sleep.

"How long are we going to wait, Charlie?"

"Give it a few more minutes!"

"What if Freddie's dead?"

The idea had crossed my mind, but that wasn't something I wanted to think about. What bothered me more was the thought that Freddie might be shanghaied and sold back into slavery. Slowly we both slid from the bed and tiptoed back to the window. This time the wax tamed the screech and while the window still fought being opened, it gradually surrendered until we both felt the cool breeze of night blow effortlessly into our room.

We climbed out onto the tin roof, closed the window quietly, and tread slowly down the incline. At the roof's edge, we put on our shoes, then dropped into the alley. No one walked around the alleys of Five Points without shoes unless they wanted to be bitten by rats or enjoyed slogging through muck. Beyond us, at the end of the alley, Little Water Street was dark. We inched toward the street, then were forced to stop abruptly, clinging to the wall, as a group of three or four Roach Guards loudly staggered toward home holding their heads and nursing sore limbs. We both held our breath. I was nearly tempted to go back when suddenly a light shined in the rear of the Reverend Caufield's flat. Not enough to illuminate the alley, the light cast just enough shadow to make David and me visible had we not dashed to the end of the alley and onto Little Water Street. Luckily, we got out before a group of men we could hear but couldn't see tramped into the alley and entered the rear of the Reverend's flat. When I looked back, the light was gone. Now, it was time to get to Robber's Alley and find Freddie.

It was a moonless night. In the near distance, the bells of police wagons rang loudly as Watchmen hauled to jail, Roachies and Black-Birders too wounded to flee. Paradise Square was emptying out, leaving small groups of disappointed onlookers drifting past smoldering bonfires as they took one last look at the field of battle before moving on to the saloons and grog shops. David and me kept to the shadows as we moved closer to the square. Across Little Water Street in the upper floor of a house occupied by Mr. Longtree, a friend of our father's, a lantern went out. I noticed that someone pulled back the curtain a little to peep unseen at the street. If it was Mr. Longtree, and he told our parents, we were finished.

"Let's make a run for it, Charlie!"

Though I wanted to say, *"Wait!"* the thought of whoever-it-was getting another minute or two to confirm their suspicion that it was David and me made the suggestion easy to follow.

"Head for the Alley," I said, rising to run straight into the square.

"No!" David had a different idea. He was heading in the opposite direction toward Cow Bay.[2]

"Dirty Ida lives on Cross Street!"

"I know, but I just saw Irish Mabel heading toward Cow Bay!"

He shot past me and into the sight of whoever-it-was peering from Mr. Longtree's window. I ran behind him with my head down. There was a light coming from Reverend Caufield's cellar, and as we passed the house again, I caught a glimpse of men huddled over a table, before someone drew a curtain over the window.

Ahead the lamp lights of Cow Bay cast disquieting glows and shadows around a cobble-stoned semi-circle of tenements and grog shops which fronted Leonard Street on its north. The street ended when it intersected with Orange. We moved quickly.

"She's headed toward Pete Williams' place I bet!"

I saw her the moment we turned the corner. Irish Mabel had hoisted herself onto an empty barrel beneath a window and was swaying to the music coming from Almacks. A crowd was gathering outside around the doors as the mob inside had ballooned to near bursting, clapping and cheering the dance competitions Pete held every other night. Fortunately, no one seemed to pay attention to David and me. As we grew closer, I put on my cap, turned it backward, stuffed my hands in my pockets and tried to act like a taildiver.[3]

"What are you doing," David snickered.

"If I act like a rogue in this crowd, no one will notice," I said.

"You look like a moron, Ringworm Charlie Little!"

It was Irish Mabel looking down from her perch on the barrel and pointing a long, teasing finger at David and me. When I heard Ringworm Charlie Little, I felt like shoving her off the empty keg and into the wall of Pete's place. Just about all the kids in Five Points had nicknames but mine came from several winters back, when I caught ringworm. If that wasn't the worst thing that ever happened to me—I had to walk around with a bald head, covered by a rag doused in the smelliest stuff you ever smelled and then be teased—it ain't worth repeatin'! A burst of applause from Pete's place took my mind off it. The crowd started whooping and hollering at whatever was going on inside. The temptation to try and look was overwhelming—even David turned toward the music for a split second.

"We're looking for Dirty Ida," I blurted out.

"Dirty *who?*"

"Ida Washington," I corrected quickly. I'd forgotten none of the girls *liked* their nicknames.

"Got no time for yah, Ringworm—can't yah see I'm watching the dance?"

59

"This is a matter of life and death, Mabel." David said it with such sincerity Irish Mabel stopped what she was doing and jumped off the barrel onto the ground.

"Whose life, Peanut?" That was David's nickname, and Irish Mabel leaned into his face, a sudden glow of curiosity and teasing behind her eyes.

"A close friend of ours!"

"Runaway, I bet—huh?" Her eyelids, like window-shades, squeezed down to narrow slits. I eased her back a little and she straightened.

"No runaway or fugitive," I put in annoyed, "he's a sailor and we think he's been shanghaied."

"Not by Roach or Black-Birder," she said. "They just fought each other, the idiots—nobody got snatched tonight!"

"Then who would do it?"

Irish Mabel had a habit of sucking her teeth whenever she was thinking. She'd make a low-pitched cluck-ing sound, and snap her fingers several times before she answered a question.

"I don't know."

"Then help us find Ida," I said. "She'll know."

"Can't you see I'm busy, Ringworm?"

At that moment, two drunken men were shoved out of Almacks and onto the street, and in the fleeting seconds that the doors were flung open, we caught a glimpse of a skinny black boy tap dancing in the center of the room, surrounded by a crowd of clapping onlook-ers and rowdy drunks. His name was Juba, a popular dancer and the rage of Five Points, where onlookers threw money at him. Everyone thought he'd wind up famous.[4]

"I was watching a jig and tap dance contest," Irish Mabel growled, "an' you two may have made me miss it!" She started to climb back onto the empty keg, when David touched her.

"Please?"

"Please? Did I hear you say, *please*, Peanut?"

"It's a matter of life and death, Mabel—life and death!"

Irish Mabel looked at David, sucked her teeth for a moment, snapped her finger, then suddenly started away from Almacks, headed toward Cross Street and the Old Brewery.

"Follow me," she said.

September 5, 1838

"It's midnight! September fifth, the year of our Lord, eighteen hundred and thirty-eight!" Without warning, a loud, roaring voice came from somewhere above us.

Is this what nighttime sounds like?

It occurred to me that neither David or me had ever been awake at this hour in our lives.

■ ■ ■

Dad would tell us later that at precisely midnight, he got out of bed and discovered we were gone. He sounded the alarm and in minutes Little Water Street was filled with freemen carrying torches and whistles.

He grabbed an old cudgel he had taken from a Black-Birder who had tried to kidnap our mother.

"Fan out over the neighborhood! My boys Charlie and David are missing! Whoever snatched them can't have gotten far! If you see 'em or anything suspicious, blow your whistles! We've got to find them!"

The men started off, leaving our mother crying in the doorway, supported by Ole'-Hit-You-With-A-Switch Moses Bowman's wife, Catherine.

"Sure hope they ain't been grabbed by them slave catchers," Catherine said shaking her head.

We were told later that neither, Ole'-Hit-You-With-A-Switch Moses Bowman or Reverend Caufield joined the men in the search.

■ ■ ■

Irish Mabel hugged the buildings on Orange Street as we hurried in single file toward Cross Street and the Old Brewery by way of Leonard Street, Cow Bay, and a narrow alley that opened onto Anthony Street. While Almacks was the loudest saloon on Orange Street, Leonard Street had several dance halls and houses of ill-repute. But Cow Bay had the most blind pigs; Jacob's Ladder, Gates of Hell and Brick Bat Mansion were the most notorious speakeasies in Five Points. Irish Mabel stopped suddenly as we approached the Gates of Hell.

"Get down," she whispered.

David and me crouched against the wall of Larry Neal's Feed Store. Up ahead, there were several young men gathered outside the Gates of Hell trying to get inside, and taunting Rosie McCann the Hot Corn girl who sold spicy ears of corn and roasted chestnuts outside the place. Everyone liked Rosie McCann. While most of the Hot Corn girls shouted out their sales pitch, Rosie sung hers:

> *Come buy my corn*
> *Come buyyy my corn*
> *Before I grow too old!*
> *Come buy my corn*
> *Don't make me mourn*
> *Spend a penny for my gold!*

Rosie was also one of the gentlest people in Five Points and largely protected by most of the men who lived here. The young men who were taunting Rosie were uptown swells just slumming.

"Uh, ohh," it was David. "Those fellas are in trouble!"

Several Shirt Tailers,[5] who had just stumbled from Eddie O'Hara's Saloon across Cow Bay took notice of the teasing and started toward the uptown swells.

"Leave her be, yah bums!" One of the Shirt Tailers shouted and charged across the Bay head first like an angry bull.

"When the fighting starts, we move," said Irish Mabel. It started at once, loud and brutal. The three of us began moving slowly across Cow Bay, trying hard not to be noticed. We stayed close to the tenements, but people began coming to their doors and windows to watch. Then as the crowd from the Diving Bell and Arcade Saloons[6] turned their attention to the fight, and men stampeded toward the brawl, we began to run in the opposite direction toward Anthony Street. David nearly tripped over a drunk who suddenly awakened. We were almost clear of Cow Bay when I saw the Tease. He was rushing around the corner from Little Water Street, his attention caught by the noise and shouting of the fight. David and me both froze; but luckily, the Tease didn't see us. He never turned in our direction. Crowds were ideal places for tail divers like the Tease. There would be a pile of wallets and valuables to lift among the spectators, and the smile on his face told me the Tease expected to do just that.

What we didn't expect was the sight of men with torches, being led by Mr. Ruggles. They were moving along Anthony Street from the far end of Paradise Square directly toward us.

"Stop, Irish!"

"What for, Ringworm? We're almost there!" Irish Mabel spun around annoyed. "And don't call me Irish again!"

"Don't call me Ringworm!" We were nose to nose.

"I don't think it's a good idea to let Mr. Ruggles catch us, Charlie." David was right.

"Who's Mr. Ruggles?"

David pointed. "He's the man leading those men with torches on the Square—they're looking for us, I betcha'."

"I know another way," Irish Mabel said and turned back toward the mêlée behind us. The fight had spilled onto both sides of Cow Bay. Some men had fallen bloodied and unconscious onto the cobblestones, others were limping to the sidelines, being helped toward opened tenement doorways by pickpockets and muggers. I was afraid we'd run smack into the Tease again—and we did! He spun around in our direction just as we turned to follow Irish Mabel.

"Hey, you gutter rats," he yelled starting in our direction. The three of us bolted with Irish Mabel leading the way toward an alley. I ran so fast my cap fell off just as we veered sharply off the street and ducked into a narrow passageway between two buildings that led to a row of wooden houses. I heard someone yell, *"Hey!"* as we followed her to a set of stairs beside the last house in what was called, Blisters Alley.

"Careful! These steps are steep!"

The staircase seemed to hurtle straight down into an impenetrable blackness.

"I can't even see them," David complained.

Irish Mabel had already taken three or four stairs on her way down.

"Get on my back." I gestured to David, "I can climb down as if the stairs are a ladder."

"Make it quick," I heard Irish Mabel whisper below me.

I stepped down the first two stairs, then turned around once David was on my back. The going was slow. There was guck on every stair, and the smell grew worse the lower we descended. When we reached the bottom, we stood still for several moments while I caught my breath and our eyes grew accustomed to the dark. We were in the dirty, rat infested, disease-ridden sewers, and I wanted to go home.

Yep!

All of a sudden I didn't care if we ever found Freddie. I looked at Irish Mabel and David and said to myself: *What am I doing here? It's after midnight—all the freemen my dad could gather are looking for David and me. We could be kidnapped at any moment by Snatch or shanghaied by Black-Birders—and, if the two of us do come out of this in one piece, I am certain to get the worst punishment my parents could ever think up!*

"Let's go," Irish Mabel said, and David and me followed, stepping in water up to our ankles, in a place where the sound of the rats rose to a loud, continuous cacophony of tortured scratches and hungry squeaks.

■　■　■

Mr. Ruggles and the freemen who accompanied him told my father that they had seen several children, two black boys and one white girl, on the other side of Paradise Square being chased by the Tease who picked up a cap, tucked it into his coat and ran when he saw the men. One of the men had yelled out to them but they had disappeared down an alley off Anthony Street. Because a free-for-all was taking place in the middle of Cow Bay, the men decided, rather than chase after the children, they would place sentinels at the corners of Mulberry, Anthony and Pearl Streets for as long as it was safe. My father didn't think it was David and me the man had seen. He decided to head toward Chatham and Pearl Streets near the City Hall.

"That's where the sham court declares freemen runaways," he said. "And that's where I'll find 'em." He was certain we'd been kidnapped.

■ ■ ■

The waters of the sewers began to recede as we moved from one passageway to another. Along some of the draining trenches, narrow ledges rose several inches above the foul-smelling liquid and we made our way carefully, like explorers, until Irish Mabel led us to another staircase. It seemed to go up six or seven stairs to a landing that bridged the trench we had been following—only we could hear voices on the other side.

"Hide!" Irish Mabel pushed us backward along the ledge. "Stay down! They sound like Birders!"

David and me crouched as low as we could without kneeling in the guck on the ledge. Irish Mabel moved forward, hugging the wall, as the voices of three men reached the landing.

"Easy, Boyo! You don't want to put too much weight on that leg, now!"

"You're both dear friends, Himus—when I get my hands on that—!"

"Calm yourself, Boyo!" The other voice interrupted. "He's always in Almacks or Terry's Fox Terrier 'T' and if not in either, driving that wagon a' his along the docks! But I'd advise yah to take a billy club with yah if you're going to try him alone, Boyo!"

Their voices began to fade. They were climbing another set of stairs slowly and with difficulty.

"Yah think I'm afraid of a buck, like Smoke?"

They had reached a door, and over the rusting screech that sounded its opening, I heard Himus say: "Of course not, Boyo, but if yah wait just a little while longer, they'll be no more Smokes left—." I think, but I can't be sure he said; "in Five Points—not a single one! They're all headed for Georgia or Alabam'!" They were both laughing as their voices disappeared. Alabam was written on the piece of paper I found on the docks!

I grabbed David's shoulder. "Did you hear what he said?"

Before David could answer, Irish Mabel was egging us forward.

"Let's go, you *like* it down here or something?"

"It's wonderful," I said, then thought, *Like a bowl of slop.*

We went over the trench and down its side to a series of tunnels through which we passed quickly before we reached a ladder. I counted seven rungs up to a trapdoor, where the constant thud of bootsteps signaled a wave of traffic above us.

"Where are we?" It was David.

"You'll see soon enough," Irish Mabel answered, tapping on the trapdoor seven times—three quick knocks, then four slower ones. The door swung open suddenly and above us stood The Turtle—Big Sue, the bouncer at Alamacks, with her mad, bulging eyes and toothless scowl. She snatched Irish Mabel up by the collar of her dress, and gestured to David and me not to move.

"What are you doing with this Staggtown trash, Mabel?"

"They're street chums, Big Sue! Set me down!" Irish Mabel was brave—even I had to admit that. "Set me down this minute!"

"I'll ask yah again. What are you doing with this trash?"

"We aren't trash," David yelled. "We're looking for a friend who's been snatched!"

Big Sue dropped Irish Mabel and turned to us annoyed. "What did you say?"

"We aren't trash," David repeated. His voice was lower this time and a bit frightened. Big Sue looked at me, both hands balled into huge stone-like knots.

"And what do *you* say, *skinny-boy?*"

I could barely get it out, and when I did, I whispered. "We aren't trash."

"Well, I think you are! And around *here* we don't let *trash* climb out of the trench!"

Suddenly, the trapdoor slammed down like an explosion, plunging David and me back into the darkness of the sewers.

■ ■ ■

*My dad would tell David and me that Big Sue had
a grudge against most of the people who lived on Little
Water Street over something that led to her sister, a
woman named Rose, being hanged in potter's field,
but when that trapdoor closed all I wanted to do was
bop her one.*[7]

■ ■ ■

Here we were, after midnight, locked out of escaping
the sewers, with no clue where Freddie was and no one to
help us. I felt like cursing, but even in the sewer I thought
my Dad would hear me and the consequence of that was
far worse than being lost. I climbed down the ladder and
looked around. There was nothing but darkness around
us—except for an area to our left where the blackness
of the tunnels seemed to gray slightly. It didn't shower
light into the passage, but as I focused in its direction
I noticed that the edges of things, corners and ceilings,
seemed to grow more distinct. It could only mean one
thing. Someone with a lamp or torch was coming, and
the moment I realized it, David started crying.

"I want to go home, Charlie!"

"Shhh! Someone's coming!"

I put my arm around his shoulders and drew him
down in a crouch. It was the first time I can remember
feeling like a big brother, with an unspoken yet understood set of responsibilities. Easing David's fear was one

of them. Making sure nothing happened to him was another. I lessened my grip on his shoulder and whispered.

"Don't worry."

Suddenly a lantern held above a man's head swung in our direction. The man holding it was Bobby Bullets Lanham, one of the ringleaders of the Black-Birders. Bullets, as he was called, had a reputation for hijacking draymen and their loads along the Bowery. A half step behind him, carrying a torch and wheezing loudly, was Pickles the Killer, a vile and evil man who was known to bite off the heads of rats. He had a standing among the slavers, grown from his uncanny ability, it was said, to pick out a fugitive slave in a crowd when no one else could.

"We're wasting our time, Bullets!" Pickles moved his torch in our direction then peered into the darkness beyond its glow. "Why would they be down here? No Staggtown pickaninny's comin' into no sewers!"

"Snatch thinks they could," Bullets said, turning away from David and me in the direction of another tunnel.

"Why do you trust a Negro who'd sell his own people?"

Bullets looked back smiling as he started away. "It's about silver, Pickles! Silver! As long as he pays I don't care one whit about his morals!"

"Do you think this raid he's plannin' will work?"

"Don't know." They moved off.

I grabbed David's arm immediately and started behind them.

"They'll catch us!"

"Not if we're quiet."

Without the lights they carried we'd never find our way out of the sewers. We had to follow the glow their torch and lantern cast. We moved slowly at first, at a considerable distance behind them. We had to wait for their lights to move off into another passageway where, if they looked back they wouldn't see us. They kept moving and we followed them until they turned into a shaft where their lights suddenly went out.

"What—?"

I covered David's mouth with my hand and froze. "Shhh!"

"I tell you I heard something!" It was Pickles.

"You've got to give up likker, Pickles, the booze has shattered your nerves my friend! First you say they're not here, now you can hear 'em? There's nothing behind us!"

For a long moment they were quiet. David and me held our breath. But lots of things were swirling in my head.

How did Snatch know David and me were missing—unless, he was one of the men with Mr. Ruggles and our dad? And what was this raid? Didn't Himus say; "They'll be no more Smokes left in Five Points—not a single one! They're all headed for Georgia or Alabam'?" And even if David and me escaped these tunnels was there time to find Freddie and warn everyone else?

"Let's go!" The lantern light glowed again and the two men began to move away from us.

David tugged at my shirt.

"They're getting away!"

"Shhh!"

Something didn't feel right. For one thing, there was only a single light now, and the noise they made slushing through the tunnel guck seemed lessened.

"Only one of them is moving," I whispered. "They're planning to trap us."

We waited for several minutes in silence when out of nowhere we heard Pickles yell.

"I hate these rats, Bullets—if those two are here let 'em stay here! I'm climbing out of these sewers—let that slave catcher come down here and find 'em himself!"

His torch glowed brightly again as he began to move. The two of us trailed him slowly until we reached the turnoff where his light began to fade.

"Didn't I tell you there was no one there?" Bullets shook his head.

Ahead there was a set of wooden stairs. Bullets was laughing and climbing upward to a landing where he disappeared into a building or hallway. There was dim light emanating from wherever the stairway led. Pickles grumbled. He stopped and gave the tunnel behind him one last gaze before he snuffed out his torch and mounted the stairs unsatisfied.

David and me took a deep breath. The way out was little more than fifteen yards away.

"Let's get out of here, Charlie!" David was ready to run to the stairs.

"We can wait," I said. I didn't trust Pickles and my hand was itching. Now that we knew where our way out was, a few more minutes wouldn't hurt. I hadn't gotten any braver, but I was getting more cautious. Hearing Snatch's name and the plan he had mentioned by two thugs made me aware that David and me couldn't allow ourselves to get caught.

My feelings about Pickles were proven right. Just before we were ready to advance, he strolled confidently to the head of the stairs and peered into the dark, hoping to see or hear something move. The only sound was the bustling and squeaking of sewer rats. Pickles' disappointment was obvious as he kicked the railing on the stairs and cursed before stalking away. In the background we could hear Bullets laughing.

"The man's daft! You can't substitute booze for proper food! How many times I got to tell you that, Pickles?"

Their voices trailed off before David and me moved. We reached the stairs, and as we climbed, the noise from whatever was beyond the landing grew louder and louder. When we reached the top, the sound from inside matched the sound in the sewers, except the chatter and noise we heard was human. I wondered if, in all the racket, we would find Freddie.

"If we don't find Freddie soon, I want to go home, Charlie," David said. He was shivering.

"Me too, but don't worry, I'll get us there." I put an arm on his shoulder. For a moment I was brave and confident, more like a big brother than I had ever felt. Then, David and me turned the corner and stepped into what could only be the Old Brewery.[8] But where on earth was Freddie?

CHAPTER FIVE

*T*HE UPROAR THAT AWAKENED ME *in Smoke's lair was filled with cursing and growls, cheers and booing that rose from moment to moment like the booming, erratic pounding of a drunken kettledrummer. Even with the door to Smoke's place shut tight the rising volume penetrated every inch of space. Smoke was gone.*

What was this hullabaloo all about? I wondered.

I made my way to the door and peeped out, careful not to open it wide enough for anyone outside to see all of me. In the near distance a crowd of mostly men, some women and exuberant boys circled a well-lit ring where, though I could not see what they were watching, I knew was a dog and rat fight. I had seen the gruesome contests in Maryland and on the waterfront. A slave owner or ship's captain might pay several boys or girls on a plantation or wharf a penny-a-piece for every rat

*they caught. They'd assemble a group of friends, build
a ring with doors standing on their sides, and chal-
lenge with bets whose dogs could kill the most rats in
a defined length of time. An ugly business, but people
inside this Brewery were flocking toward the battle. The
fox terriers waiting outside the circle were impatient.
They were itching to fight. Snarling and growling, they
strained their leashes to near breaking as they charged
at boys who teased and goaded them as they passed.*[1]
*As I watched the spectators, I recognized Pickles the
Killer as he and another man greeted the Tease then
strolled around the crowd looking for a place they could
squeeze through to get closer to the fighting. I noticed
around the gathering that the inside of the Brewery was
a dark, partially open space reaching five stories into
the air. As my eyes grew accustomed to the darkness,
and though I had heard their voices when I opened the
door, I could make out dark figures above me, shouting
and yelling down at the fight ring. In all my days as a
cook's mate I had never heard language so vile. I closed
the door to Smoke's den, sat down in the only chair,
and tried to decide what I would do next. I had to find
the man named David, as impossible as it seemed, and
despite the help that Smoke had given, my memory of
the friend I had met made me wary of everyone. At
that moment, I realized that being free in New York
or any other northern city wasn't simply a matter of
escaping from the South. As long as slavery existed,
to be free, one had always to be vigilant. Suddenly the
door swung open, and in walked a young lady. Terrified*

*when she saw me, she stepped back instantly against
the opened door frame.*

"Who are you?"

*"Smoke Newsom saved my life this evening and
brought me here to escape capture. My name is Freddie
Johnson, cook's mate on the S.S. Mullens, Ma'am."
I said it quickly hoping she wouldn't panic and start
screaming. Surprisingly, she seemed more annoyed with
Smoke than troubled by me. An attractive woman, she
removed her coat and unafraid, crossed the den placing
it neatly on a corner shelf.*

*"I'm Smoke's sister, Mariah, and I'm afraid you're
going to have to leave," she said. "As usual he didn't tell
me anything about you, and in these dangerous times,
I'm afraid I can't let you stay here, Mr.—?"*

"Johnson!"

*"Mr. Johnson, there's talk of a raid on freemen about
to happen here in Five Points. You must leave. Now!"*

*"How," I asked her, "if a man is free, can he be
sold back into slavery?"*

*"One of our own leads the raids, Sir—please, you
must go—if they come we can't be seen harboring
strangers!" She was clearly frightened.*

*I was to find out that the Black-Birders and slave
catchers who formed the New York Kidnapping Club,
aided by the ruthless City Recorder Riker, were preparing to snatch as many freemen as they could. They
would then sell them and send them back to the South.[2]*

*I thanked her for not screaming and slipped from
Smoke's lair and onto the first floor of the cavernous*

Old Brewery called, The Den of Thieves. Though I was alone again, I felt relieved. Despite being saved by Smoke, the atmosphere in New York was laced with fear and I wanted to escape it. If the kindly Mariah Newsom had screamed when she entered, I realized I might have struck her to save myself.

"Lord, where was the David I was told to find?"

■ ■ ■

When we crept into the Old Brewery, measuring each step amid the din of barking dogs and rooting people, the first words we heard came from Dirty Ida. Standing on a platform in the middle of four older women who ignored us, as they strained to see what the crowd in the distance was cheering on, Dirty Ida yelled down at David and me with a nonchalance that gave me the impression that she knew where we were all along and was waiting for us.

"It's about time, Ringworm," she said.

I was really mad. *She knew where we were and did nothing to find us or help us out of the tunnels?*

"Why didn't you—?"

Suddenly she disappeared. David grabbed my arm.

"Where did she go, Charlie?"

I looked around. The inside of the Old Brewery was huge. Above us were five stories of what could be called living lairs. They surrounded a large, square opening connected by ladders, ropes and partial staircases in the center of the building. From what I could tell, each lair was occupied by different groups of people or families, and guarded by dogs. On the ground floor, where we stood, huge wooden vats once used to ferment beer had been converted into lairs with makeshift doors of wood or canvas. The entire floor was covered with sawdust and trash.

"What took you so long?" Dirty Ida was behind us, smiling.

"Did you know where we were?" I was furious.

Dirty Ida shrugged. "Mabel told me to watch out for you."

I had forgotten about Mabel, and sputtered on, "We were down in the tunnels with no torch—!"

"Ida, do you know where our friend is," David interrupted.

"Nope! But Bullets Lanham and Pickles are looking for you two, and if I don't hide you and Peanut, Ringworm, you're liable to be shanghaied and sold the (so-and-so) down South—so be (so-and-so) careful how you speak to me!"

I felt like strangling Dirty Ida, but when I looked at David and quickly assessed our circumstances—mainly that our father would, *if* we got home, more than likely take his belt to our hides and give us the whipping of the *century*—*and*, as long as we were inside the Old Brewery, Ida was our only way to safety, I relented. After all, wasn't it my duty to protect my brother first, no matter what?

Dirty Ida gazed at me with an innocent smile on her face and sighed. It was the same look she had in school whenever she knew the answer to a question that no one else knew.

"Follow me," she said, and started toward a ladder. David and me followed, climbing up rung by rung until we reached the second floor of the Brewery. Dirty Ida said she lived on the fourth floor, but when we reached the second floor there was no ladder, rope or partial set of stairs that reached up to the third floor. We would have to make our way to a dark corner of the second floor where a Keeper only allowed residents of the upper floors to pass beyond the second floor for free—everyone else had to pay! Neither David or me had a penny to our names, but added to the petty larceny of the price-to-go-up, we still had to pick our way past lairs, where a few families slept, while others gambled, argued or conducted business our parents thought we children were not supposed to know about. And, to make matters worse, every lair was guarded by a dog! We could see their eyes glowing at the dark edges of each lair. Two or three dogs stirred as we approached. David grabbed my shirt and held on tightly as Dirty Ida moved toward the first dog, a yapping mutt she smiled at and gently called, King Edward.

"Behave, King Edward, it's just me, Ida. Aren't we friends?"

King Edward's tail wagged as he lowered his head into Dirty Ida's hands.

"They're all named after the (so-and-so) Kings of England," she laughed, and moved forward.

I must admit my opinion of Dirty Ida changed that night. As foul-mouthed as she could be, she never used a curse word or swore at the animals. Every dog along the way seemed to know her and each time we approached another lair, Dirty Ida would charm the animals into gentleness—except when we reached the last one. The final lair was presided over by a Keeper and surrounded by a large black canvas sheet, cut from a sail that hid the stairs leading to the third floor. Before we reached it, Dirty Ida told us that each day the Keeper was replaced, so that everyone living in the Old Brewery would have a chance to earn a few pennies by keeping the money they charged slummers and drunks.[3]

When Dirty Ida opened the canvas to peep into the last lair, the Bandog[4] charged the slit, barking and straining the leash until the Keeper, One-eye Jolly Dunbar, managed to hobble down the stairs and quiet the animal. One-eye had an old fighting scar from the center of his forehead to a place on his cheek, below where his right eye had been. Scruffy, toothless and cranky, he was an old man, gone lame from too many battles and too little care.

"Best guard dog in the Brewery," One-eye said. The dog continued to growl and One-eye rapped him with his cane. "Shut up, King Henry! An' don't let me speak ta' you agin'! Hea' me?" King Henry lowered his head and stalked toward the rear of the lair where he laid down. "That'll be two pennies, boys." One-eye held out his hand. Tied to a piece of leather around his wrist was a small cloth bag with coins inside it. It was the same kind of canvas bag I'd fished out of the Hudson—with the same smiling skull drawn on it!

"Mr. One-eye, these are friends of mine—."

Before Dirty Ida could finish I blurted out, "Where'd you get that canvas bag?" I pointed at the smiling skull.

One-eye yanked his hand back. "What's it to yah, twerp?"

I noticed King Henry rose slowly and stared in our direction.

"Mr. One-eye, my brother fished a bag like that out of the river, and we think the owner of that bag was kidnapped!" David said. "Do you know anything about it?"

"You twerps accusing ole' One-eye of stealin'?"

"No, Sir," I said, nudging David closer to the stairs as King Henry began to move one hesitant step at a time toward us. Dirty Ida had noticed the dog as well. She took a step toward the stairs.

"Did someone give it to you?"

"Nobody gave One-eye nothin'! This fell out de' pocket of a slave catcher prob'ly on his way back south by now! They put stuff belongin' ta' the folks they catch in these bags!" He shook his head as though he felt sorry for the person whose stuff had been in the bag. My heart sank. The report of the Cullen children had been true; Buster and Mattie had been kidnapped after all. I felt so sorry for them.

"Could you tell us on which ship the slave catcher sailed," I asked, inching ever closer to the stairs. Dirty Ida was on the bottom step, moving and reaching for David's hand as he climbed up to join her. By now King Henry was almost directly behind One-eye Jolly Dunbar, and from what part of his open jaws I could see, itching to strike and tear someone's arm off—mine!

"Where's my two pennies," One-eye hissed, reaching his hand out again.

I froze, telling myself, *if I have to, I'll gladly sacrifice my life for my brother and let this flesh-eating monster, King Henry, tear me to bits!* I could see my coffin being carried through the streets of Five Points as my classmates removed their caps and waved goodbye.

"Two, or you two goes nowhea'!"

"These are my cousins, Mr. One-eye," Dirty Ida said.

"You said they was your friends—You' lyin'!" One-eye glared at Dirty Ida. "I knows your whol' family Ida, and these two ain't part of 'em!"

"They are *so*," she shouted back at him.

I took a deliberate step toward Dirty Ida and David, not turning my back on King Henry but moving with the confidence I was sure a relative would show. Where I got the bravery, I'll never know. King Henry growled and Dirty Ida took off like a rabbit with David behind her.

"Get 'em, Henry! Rip that 'un ta' bits!"

King Henry charged me at once. I shot up the stairs as the dog leaped as high into the air as he could, nearly biting my left foot an instant before the leash around his neck tightened and halted his momentum. He fell backward, trying to break his fall by twisting away from the stairs, only to land on something that hurt him. I never saw what it was. I heard him howl, his painful bellow rising above the angry shouts of One-eye Jolly Dunbar.

"Yah dumb mutt! Yah let 'em git away!"

I felt sorry for King Henry, but I couldn't turn back. We were running toward the opposite end of the third floor where the next way-up awaited us. It was David that slowed us down. This floor, unlike the floor below us, was raucous. Brighter, the light from each lair spilled into a narrow pathway that snaked between and around the speakeasies, grog shops and private stalls that covered the floor. When David spoke I barely heard him.

"Wait! What about Freddie?" He stopped. "We've got to find him!"

"Didn't you hear Mr. One-eye," Dirty Ida was leaning into David's face. "Your friend's probably been shanghaied by now and carried south!"

"What Mr. One-eye said doesn't mean Freddie was caught—and if he was, maybe Mr. One-eye knows who took him."

"I ain't goin' back—remember, Mabel said someone's looking for you and Ringworm!"

I stepped forward. As much as I admired Dirty—I'd call her Ida from now on. *It's the least I could do for someone who had saved my life.*

"We can't let the slave catchers take him back south, Ida," I said, "everybody deserves to be free. Everybody. And my name's Charles."

"And mine's David!"

Ida closed her eyes for one long moment. When she opened them they were wide and round—like two angry lights bulging from her forehead.

"Well, Charles," she said my name like a cuss word. "You and David want this Freddie so bad, you find him your (so-and-so) self!"

"Fine! Just tell us how to get out of here," I grumbled back at her.

Ida smiled like a well-fed cat. "Well now, that's a problem isn't it?" She crossed her arms over her chest and put several fingers under her chin the way Ole'-Hit-You-With-A-Switch Bowman did sometimes at school.

"Hmm, seems to me you two are faced with a dilemma," she mimicked Ole'-Hit-You-With-A-Switch, "dear, dear, what shall you do?" She then lifted her eyes toward the heavens like a prank-inspired saint.

"Would you *please* tell us, Ida?" David pleaded. I suddenly realized that seeing the bag around One-eye Jolly Dunbar's wrist had changed David. I wanted to toss Ida back down the stairs. Instead I grabbed David's arm and pulled him away.

"Let's go! We'll find our own way out! We don't beg anybody!"

David was reluctant but he followed as I started toward a lair with the brightest lights. I was so angry I was boiling inside. Suddenly, just as we approached a grog shop, a big, heavy-set, light-skinned woman, who looked familiar, was shoved out of the shop into our path. She stumbled, but bumped into me as the man who pushed her stood at the edge of the grog shop, calling her names I won't repeat. Righting herself, she cursed him back, then turned, looked down at me and slurred gently, "Thank you, youngun', you a sport if I eva' seen one!" Turning again with great caution, she started away, taking each step like a deer on thin ice. Her sympathetic demeanor didn't last long, however.

"*Idaaa!*" The heavy-set woman was screaming, her voice booming.

Behind David and me, Ida was moving toward the woman slowly, fearfully. Her hands, up around her shoulders, were together, rubbing nervously over one another, as though preparing to ward off some terrible something I could not imagine. It came swiftly though. The woman snatched Ida by the shoulder and slapped her hard across the face screaming; "*Whea's my money, you bugger? Whea's my money?*" Before Ida could answer she started shaking her and it was then that I recognized her. She was Ida's mother, Mrs. Dot Washington, who everyone called Princess Dorothy,[5] a woman I had seen talking to our mother outside church.

"*Whea' is it?*"

Poor Ida was crying and screaming so intensely she couldn't answer her mother.

"*Whea'?* Been out all day sweepin' crossings—how much you make?"

"She was saving us, Princess Dorothy," David shouted.

"She was, Mrs. Washington," I chimed in rushing toward them as Princess Dorothy turned around freezing a slap she was about to give Ida in mid air.

"And who is you two?"

"We're Mrs. Little's sons, Ma'am—I'm Charles and this is my brother David. We met you at church!"

Princess Dorothy threw her head back, looked down her short nose and gradually—very gradually—began to smile. Her entire demeanor changed and her booming voice gave way to a softer, more elegant sound.

"Your mamma is a generous spirit," she said and stopped, shaking her head sadly as she stared down at the floor. "But don't y'all eva' call me Princess Dorothy again, you hea' me?"

"Yes Ma'am," I said. She was still slightly lubricated, and something she seemed to be remembering suddenly spilled from her and made her cry.

"When my Hamel went missin', your mamma 'n daddy was the only ones in de' Points helped me an' my five out!" Ida was the youngest of five children. Her father, a freeman, had been kidnapped, sold into slavery and never found, way back in 1826 when Ida was an infant. Mrs. Washington put a hand to her eyes, then dried them on her sleeve. "She *saved* you, you say?"

"Yes Ma'am," I said quickly, "an' she was just showing us another way out of the Brewery." Ida's head snapped up, glaring at me with a cold menace.

"We're looking for a friend who was kidnapped," David put in.

"Well, you'd betta' git back home quick, 'cause tonight's de night the Kidnappin' Club is fixin' ta' grab the bigges' package a runaways eva'!" She put her hand to her mouth, bent forward and whispered, "An' they won't all be runaways eitha'! A lots gonna' be unsuspectin' freemen! That's all they talkin' 'bout in the grog shops!" She straightened. "I sure don't want yo'r mamma to be worryin' 'bout you. Ida— show them the otha' way out—tonight, ain't nobody on the first floor safe. Now you all go right home, you hea' me?"

"Yes Ma'am," I said.

Princess Dorothy gestured to Ida to direct us. "Go on, now! Show 'em!"

Ida nodded and started away quietly without looking at David or me. I knew she was still angry even though I wasn't entirely sure why. All I could think of was, *What happened to Freddie?*

■ ■ ■

Freddie said; "Most of the crowd hustling across The Den of Thieves toward the dog fight were enjoying themselves. Likker passed from hand to hand, and the sound of laughter and joking was everywhere. No separation of the races or men from women in the Old Brewery. The dog fights brought all together. To these poor creatures this was entertainment—a way of casting off the work and trials of their days. While I still believe nothing is more cruel than enslaving another human being, I learned that close on the heels of unjust servitude—poverty and ignorance are equal drains on a nation's well-being. I had no idea what I would do once I left Smoke's, but the matter was decided for me, as a good-humored party of three women and two men grabbed my arm and pulled me along with them as they mingled with the spectators. I searched the crowd looking for Smoke, but it was Pickles the Killer's high-pitched howl that caught my attention. He was standing with the Tease and the man I would later find out was Bobby Bullets, several rows in front of me, taking bets on the rats and dog from all comers. I lowered my head when Pickles suddenly spun around and screeched; "Bet on the dogs all you want mates, but the rats will run 'em ragged!"

"You say!" One of the women standing with me yelled. "I'm betting on Fido, Pickles!" She passed two coins down to the Tease.

"I'll stand with the lady—such as she is!" A big, red-faced fellow on the other side of the crowd shouted and dissolved into laughter as he tossed his coins at Bobby Bullets.

"Since when did rats start betting against themselves," the Lady roared back.

The spectators were in stitches laughing until a dark-gray, brown-nosed rat, nearly the size of a large kitten, bit the dog on its side and the animal let out an awful yowl.

"*What did I say,*" *shrieked Pickles laughing. "Pay up, yah bumpkins—pass the money my way! That rat's got your dog trembling!*"

The dog may have been bitten but it was far from being defeated. It reared up on its hind legs and sprang at the rat, snatching it by the neck and—I didn't see the kill. The sight of the bloody ring filled with rat carcasses and the bleeding dog had turned my stomach. But as I spun away and heard the crowd cheering I caught a flash of recognition in the face of the Tease. Looking in my direction he nudged Bobby Bullets, pointed at me, and said something to him. I started away from the crowd at once, and instantly heard the rapid ringing of a warning bell.

"*Slave catchers!*"

The spectators around me scattered, melting away in a few seconds into small groups and individuals running for their lives. Two large shipping doors had swung open, and Black-Birders led by the notorious team of Daniel Nash and Elias Boudinot, with a black man in a handkerchief mask, who I assumed was Snatch, and carrying a 2-foot-long truncheon, burst in the Old Brewery. Snatch pointed out people at random. They grabbed one of the men that befriended me at once. I bolted toward a ladder in the center of the building, that as I ran, was slowly being pulled up.

"*Hold it! Stop!*"

■ ■ ■

The instant Ida started away David and me heard the warning bell ring. Suddenly everyone was yelling "slave catchers!" and running in all directions. Princess Dorothy straightened, rushed to Ida, grabbed her hand and told us to follow her. We started back toward the large hole in the third floor.

■ ■ ■

But Freddie told us; "I reached the hole just as the man and a woman I could barely see above me tossed the ladder onto the second floor. The man's gestures told me he was sorry, but had no choice. The woman disappeared. Suddenly I heard Smoke yell "Freddie!"

■ ■ ■

David heard Smoke call Freddie's name just as we passed the hole. He turned back toward it and looked down, pointing. Princess Dorothy let Ida go and rushed into a lair.

"*Freddie*," David yelled and pointed. "It's him Charlie!"

■ ■ ■

Freddie looked up. "I knew it was David and you above me, but two Black-Birders had jumped Smoke and he needed my help. I lunged toward them, grabbing

one and tossing him away from Smoke who was pound-
ing another attacker senseless. A short, muscular man
struck me with a cudgel that nearly deadened my arm.
I swung at him as hard as I could and knocked him
down and was struck by Snatch. I glimpsed three men
pounce on Smoke as Snatch hit me again. I tore off
his mask as I tumbled, unconscious, to the floor of the
Old Brewery. I saw Snatch's face for the first time, a
second before everything went black."

■ ■ ■

David wanted to go after Freddie, but I pulled him
away from the hole as the man who was obviously
Snatch aimed his bludgeon in our direction, covering
his face.

Who was he?

"Get up there and grab those children," Snatch
shouted.

We started away at once, but Ida turned back
toward the way-up where One-eye Jolly Dunbar and
King Henry were waiting.

"I'm not going back down that way-up," I said
stopping.

"There's another way-up, *stupid*," Ida sneered, "if
we go to the fourth floor way-up at the end of this floor
they'll catch us for sure!"

"Us?"

"You heard me," she said. "I've decided to run
away."

"Why," David asked.

Ida didn't answer. She was moving toward one of the lairs close to the opening of the second floor way-up and One-eye Jolly Dunbar. We could hear Snatch and his slave-catching friends hollering for the ladder to the second floor to be dropped. The lair before us was dark and seemed empty, though I felt someone, or something, that breathed was inside as we moved slowly toward vague outlines of boxes, storage baskets and barrels stacked along the lair's walls.

"Grab my hand, Peanut, and do exactly what I do," Ida whispered, extending a hand I could barely see toward David.

"Why," David asked, and immediately bumped into a barrel that tipped on its edge and for a moment threatened to tumble.

"That's why," she replied. Her encounter with her mother hadn't cooled her mouth. She twisted sideways and shimmied forward into a narrow crevice between several stacks of barrels and baskets. Outside the lair I could hear Snatch and his men running and shouting toward the second floor way-up, as I slid sideways and followed Ida. Beyond the crevice was an abandoned chute and beside it a large wooden door leading to the outside of the Old Brewery. Ida went to the door but couldn't pull it open.

"Lend a hand, Ringworm!"

"If you call David and me another name, Ida," I said, crossing my arms over my chest, "we can all wait right here and get caught!"

I looked at David and he crossed his arms over his chest as well. Ida's eyes narrowed into two slits again, and her face pinched itself into a squinchie, crushed-paper expression that defied naming. She turned back to the door.

"Alright, *Charles!*"

David and me smiled at one another as we both grabbed at the door's handle and yanked it open.

"Is there another way-up," I asked Ida, gasping at what lay before us.

"You can go back inside, *Charles*," she smiled mockingly.

The night sky was still dark and starless. The wooden door had opened onto what had been the landing of an outside set of stairways that permitted Old Brewery workers to get from floor to floor should the chutes on the inside of the building slow down or clog up for whatever reason during the beer-making process. The first and second-floor stairways were gone, as well as the landing between the door and the stairway to the fourth floor. We would have to jump from the sill of the doorway to the rickety bannister of the stairway. If we missed, or the bannister or stairs gave way, we'd fall to a certain death three stories down to the cobblestone alley below.

"You go first, *Charles*," Ida said as she gestured *after you!* and bowed mocking. "You can catch *David* when he leaps, but once you do, run up as fast as you can, the third-floor stairway is pretty rickety!"

"What about you?"

"I've done it before, *Charles,*" Ida said.

I took a deep breath and leaped. Surprised that I landed on the first step of the third-floor stairway, I turned around, smiling nervously and triumphantly at David and Ida. I grabbed the bannister and reached out to David.

"Come on, there's nothing to it!"

David took two steps back, then bolted forward and jumped. I caught his hand and yanked him onto the step just as the stairway groaned a little and pulled ever so slightly away from the Old Brewery wall.

"Run up to the landing! Quickly!"

David took the stairs two at a time. Once he reached the top I turned back to Ida. The look on her face shocked me. Ida was terrified.

"I don't have to come with you—those (so-and-so's) are not looking for me!"

"Idaaa—can't you hear them?"

Behind her I could hear King Henry barking wildly in the midst of shouts from One-eye Jolly Dunbar.

"They're not going to let you escape! You want to be a slave?"

The voices were getting closer. Ida looked back for a second, then closed her eyes and leaped with both her hands out. I caught her right hand but the force of her weight loosened the rotted wooden supports. The bannister cracked and tore away from several stairs as the third-floor stairway began to give way. It was all both of us could do to reach the fourth floor before the entire set of stairs fell from the outer wall, hurling wood, brick and mortar down into the alley. The noise brought Pickles and a man I recognized as Daniel Nash, a slave catcher, to the open doorway.

"They're some of 'em up above!" Nash was pointing at us as we took the fourth-floor stairway to the top of the Old Brewery and climbed over the roof ledge.

What now?

CHAPTER SIX

*O*UR DAD TOLD US: *he heard the warning bell the moment it rang and headed back toward Little Water Street at once. Black-Birders had been known to break into the houses of freemen and kidnap women and children if the men were gone. He ran down Chatham Street to Pearl where he saw Ole'-Hit-You-With-A-Switch Moses Bowman turning the corner of Cross Street and running in his direction, waving his arms.*

"It's the slave catchers, Robert. They're raiding the Old Brewery!"

Ole'-Hit-You-With-A-Switch stopped in front of Dad panting, bending over, his hands on both knees. He looked up, exhausted.

"You left the women alone, Moses?"

If Ole'-Hit-You-With-A-Switch answered, our dad didn't have time to respond. He was racing toward Little Water Street leaving Ole'-Hit-You-With-A-Switch to follow him. When he reached Cross Street he saw a group of men with torches heading toward Little Water Street. He wasn't sure if it was David Ruggles and men from the Vigilance Committee. They were leaving Paradise Square and helping someone who appeared injured. He stopped behind them hugging the wall of the Newkirk Nailhouse and blew his whistle. Two men stopped and blew their whistles to answer him.

"Is that a signal," Ole'-Hit-You-With-A-Switch asked, trying to catch up to our dad who ignored him.

"Robert Little—permission to come forward! My wife and the women with her are alone!"

"Step into the light, Robert Little."

"Come forward, Robert." Mr. Ruggles saw him immediately and our dad rushed past him and onto Little Water Street.

"What about me?" asked Ole'-Hit-You-With-A-Switch.

"Stop where you are," one of the men said, raising a club.

"I'm the schoolteacher, Moses Bowman!"

By then, our dad was inside, climbing the stairs to our rooms. Mr. Ruggles was beside him.

"Open the door Alice! It's me, Robert!"

Inside, our mother slid a chest to one side, then yanked the door open and rushed into our dad's arms. She told him several minutes after Ole'-Hit-You-With-A-Switch left to find our dad and Mr. Ruggles, the Black-Birders ran through the street trying all the doors and forcing several that were not locked. They hauled Grandpa Jackson from his third-floor room, put shackles on his wrists, and marched him away. They caught Vincent the Gash as he staggered out of a dive on Orange Street. Junkman Tyler Lewis would have been snatched were it not for his three daughters, Elizabeth, Mary and Victoria, who heard him screaming and beat up the Black-Birders who tried to grab him.

"Why did Moses leave?" Mr. Ruggles asked Bowman's wife, Catherine, once he was inside.

"He wanted to warn y'all," she justified.

"But his job was to watch you!" Our dad was angry. Mr. Ruggles touched his shoulder just as Ole'-Hit-You-With-A-Switch knocked on the front door below. It calmed him a bit.

"It's me, Moses, let me in!" Trimmer Spurts opened the door and he entered.

Our dad told us he didn't explode on Ole'-Hit-You-With-A-Switch because he had a strange feeling about the man—something he wanted to discuss with Mr. Ruggles—something an argument with the teacher would have prevented. Ole'-Hit-You-With-A-Switch collected his wife Catherine and left. Our dad told Mr. Ruggles he was going back to Chatham Street to search for us, but the signal of 'friend or foe' would be changed from two short whistles to a single clap of the hands.

"Why, Robert?"

"A precaution, Ruggles," he said. "A precaution."

Ida, David, and me had reached the roof of the Old Brewery, but we had to find a way down before the slave catchers reached the fifth floor and the trapdoor that led to where we were. To the east of the Old Brewery was the Brennan Grain and Liquor Company[1] but its roof was slanted and slippery. Jumping onto it would have assured the three of us broken legs or worse, if we slid down its length and fell to the ground. We treaded step by step along the edge of the Old Brewery roof, looking for anything that would provide a safe way down. Below us on Cross Street, Black-Birders were marching four men and two women in shackles from the Old Brewery, east, across the bottom of Paradise Square toward Orange Street, just as a company of six Watchmen turned onto Cross from Mulberry Street. One of the men could have been Freddie, but we were too far away to be sure. The Watchmen did nothing to interfere with the Black-Birders, even though one of the women cried out that she knew two of them and was not a fugitive.

"You know me Larry Burns! You too, Matthew Taylor! It's me, Annie Drumond! You all know I ain't no runaway! Don't let 'em do me like this! Oh God, it's me, Larry! Matty? Matty, it's meee!"

"Where are they taking them," David asked Ida.

"The Leatherheads? Probably to Send-'em-South Riker, the judge—he decides who is and who isn't a runaway."[2]

That was all Ida said. At that moment something or someone hit the trapdoor to the roof. Then hit it again.

Even from where we were we could hear the door and the latch begin to give. The next blow would tear the door from its hinge. We had to get off the roof! There was a drain pipe at the rear of the building that hung halfway down the side of the Brennan Grain and Liquor Company. The drop from the bottom of the pipe to the roof wasn't two stories, but that corner of the Brennan Grain and Liquor Company was right above a section of Murderer's Alley piled high with heaps of garbage and trash tossed from the roof and open windows of the Old Brewery. It not only looked menacing in the darkness, but its acrid smell was sickening.

"Me, first?" David and Ida were both looking at me. So, I climbed onto the pipe just as the trapdoor flew off its hinge. It scared me and I dropped at least ten feet before I stopped my fall. I kicked my feet up against the brick wall and skidded to the bottom of the pipe and let go. Bloosh! The pile of garbage gave way like a thick, foul-smelling pool of dead rat and dog guts. Agghh! Behind me, David and Ida also landed in the muck. But I was so nauseous, I leaped up instantly, plowing my way out of the stench. I stumbled to the edge of the alley before I heard shouts from the Black-Birders above us.

"We'll get you before this night's over," Pickles yelled. "Before it's over, you brazen cockroaches!"

Ida turned around and called Pickles a name I won't repeat. We gathered our smelly selves and headed out to Cross Street.

"Where are we going, Charlie?" It was David.

"To the court; that's where they take the ones they catch!"

"We're kids, nobody will listen to us," he said.

The remark stopped us cold. David was right. In the court someone would be paid to swear everyone who was caught was a runaway, then the city recorder, Riker, would authorize them to be deported to the South immediately and sent back to their so-called legal slave owners. There was also a good chance, if we showed up in the court, we'd be arrested and sold into slavery ourselves.

"Ida!"

Irish Mabel was standing with Two-tooth Clarabella Osbourn and a group of Old Brewery tenants who had witnessed the raid and were lucky enough not to be caught. She ran over, but froze before she hugged Ida.

"My God, Lady Guinevere, you stink!"

Lady Guinevere?

"We're running from Pickles, Mabel," Ida barked. She hated being dirty and the idea that she smelled like Murderer's Alley made her slightly sick.

"Don't worry about him—him and Bobby Bullets may never get out of the Brewery," Irish Mabel laughed. "They hurt King Henry and you can't hurt Brewery dogs and get away with it."

By the time Pickles and his friends reached the street we will be long gone, I thought. *Serves them right!*

"Your momma's looking for you, Ida," Irish Mabel nearly whispered it. "She was crying."

"I don't have a (so-and-so) momma!" Ida said it angrily and walked away. David and me joined her.

"Rein in your horses, Lady. Where are y'all going?" Two-tooth Clarabella walked forward trying to stay out of *smell range*. She covered her nose as she approached. "Y'all smell like last years bloomers! Wheww!" Two-tooth had a deep southern accent. Her Momma had come north from Alabam' with a Daddy who gambled and was shot dead in a green-grocer's liquor house. Through sewing and several things kids weren't supposed to know about, she managed to eek out a living in Five Points and send Two-tooth to school.

The Watchmen were gone now, and though we hadn't said anything to one another, we were heading in the direction we saw the Black-Birders take their captives.

"Were going after a friend who was kidnapped," I said. "The Black-Birders went up Orange Street."

"Do you know *where* they went?" It was Irish Mabel with her arms crossed over her chest.

"They're more than likely taking them to the Court, Mabel," Ida answered.

Irish Mabel started sucking her teeth and shaking her head, no. "The Court won't open 'til eight in the morning! I betcha' they stash 'em overnight in Rag-Picker Judson's Saloon on Leonard Street. It's a Black-Bird hideout."

"Y'all will neva' git 'em out of there," Two-tooth opined. "Unless y'all have some help!"

"Like what," David asked. He moved toward Two-tooth but she three-stepped backward.

"You don't have to be close ta' talk ta' me, Peanut!"

"My name is not Peanut, Two-tooth!"

"What'd you call me?" Despite how we smelled Two-tooth was ready to pop David.

"No more nicknames!" I yelled, and my volume startled Two-tooth. She halted dead in her tracks. "Our *friend* has been kidnapped, Clarabella! How can we *help him?*"

Two-tooth glared at me for a long moment, then said looking at everyone, "We'll call out the Magus!"

"It's too late," Irish Mabel said. "Everyone's asleep!"

"Not everybody." She turned to Ida. "Why don't y'all go on up ta' Rag-Picker Judson's Saloon and git the lay of the land, and me and Mabel will bring the Magus and meet y'all in Cow Bay."

■ ■ ■

Freddie let us know, "*It took four men to subdue Smoke. Two men hit him with truncheons on his arms and shoulders, while one man got down on his knees behind him and the last man tripped Smoke backward over the third man and onto the ground. I recognized one of the men as a Black-Birder who chased us into the tunnels. Their boss walked over smiling, hands on his hips. Snatch was gone when I awakened.*

"*Yah didn't think we'd ever get you, did you, devil?*" *He started laughing and ridiculing Smoke as* two men shackled Smoke's hands in front of him, and yanked him upright. "See? It don't take much to subdue these monkeys!"

"You won't hold me long Danny Nash," Smoke said, out of breath, "and you'll be lucky if you live through the night!" He turned to me. "Don't worry, Freddie, we'll get out of this."

"Look who's talking," Nash said incredulous. "You got some secret trick under your shirt?"

Smoke stared at Nash silently. At that moment I began to truly admire Smoke. Here he was, shackled and subdued, but completely composed, defiant, threatening and certain he'd escape. He unnerved Nash who, waving his cap, gestured to his men to move us at once.

"Add these two to the rest of the vermin—and God help the man that let's them escape!"

They led us cautiously but swiftly out of The Den of Thieves by way of Murderer's Alley, where another shackled man, oldish and bearded, was shoved into the group. He was introduced to us by Nash as Mr. Hoggard and he needed a cane to walk.

"A poor Negro runaway for ten years," Nash smiled, "you should have known—sooner or later, the great Danny Nash would send your devilish butt back where you came from!" Hoggard said nothing.

I would find out later that Smoke's sister Mariah had nearly become a captive herself when the crowd watching the dog and rat fight began to scatter once the warning bell rang. Worried after I left, she began looking for Smoke in The Den of Thieves. Terrified *at the idea of being kidnapped and caught between the slave catchers and her lair, she climbed the ladder to the second floor and helped to pull it up just as I reached it. She hid with a friend until Pickles and the slave catchers made their way to the third floor hunting for David and you. It was Mariah who made sure Pickles and the men with him got trapped on the third floor. When she saw a desperate One-eye Jolly Dunbar carrying a wounded King Henry and begging for help, she incited anger in the second floor people of the Old Brewery. They collected around the way-up and threatened to pound Pickles into dust if he came down. Nobody mistreated Old Brewery guard dogs. That same anger had begun to filter through The Den of Thieves slightly ahead of Nash rushing us out of the Old Brewery. We joined the others outside the Old Brewery and were marched past a group of Watchmen, up Orange Street to Leonard, then shoved down an alley outside Rag-Picker Judson's Saloon. At the rear of the place a Birder unlocked a back door and led us into a windowless, cell-like room.*

"Don't worry," he said smiling, "you won't be here long; by tomorrow you'll be sailing peacefully down South where a wonderful life of slavery awaits each one of you vermin!"

Laughing, he locked us in, leaving two men outside as lookouts.

One poor woman couldn't stop crying. Annie Drummond was heartbroken that several of the Watchmen had pretended not to know her.

"There's not a week goes by they ain't in my place drinkin'," she said. "Not a week in the last three or four years! How could they do that? I'm a free woman and nobody's slave!" She shouted it at the locked door. "A free woman, yah hear me? Born free!"

Smoke calmed her.

"Annie, just think about your children and getting out of here to be with them," he said.

She was quiet for a while but it was hard to see how anyone in our situation could think of anything else but escaping.

■ ■ ■

Orange Street was quiet. The raid had emptied or shuttered most of the saloons and grog houses. Only a few die-hard drunks remained outside and we easily passed them and headed to Cow Bay and Leonard Street. Rag-Picker Judson's place looked onto Cow Bay from the north side of Leonard Street. It was still open but only two sloshed revelers outside staggered away from its double doors. Inside, an old fiddler managed the final notes of Long Ago,[3] then abruptly stopped playing. Ida, David and me were creeping cautiously along the dark edge of the closed shops that bordered Cow Bay. When the music stopped, we froze.

"What do you think," Ida asked.

I didn't have time to answer. At that moment Irish Mabel and Two-tooth Clarabella appeared behind us. I nearly jumped out of my skin.

"Where's the Magus?"

The two girls looked at each other sadly.

"They're not coming," Two-tooth Clarabella said.

"Why?"

Irish Mabel sucked her teeth, and breathed deeply several times before the words exploded from her. "They said they won't help runaway slaves escape!"

"I don't like it either, Ida," Two-tooth added. "My momma would whip me all over Five Points if she thought I was helpin' some fugitive escape his masta' or missus!"

"Men ain't supposed to have *masters*," I said.

"Freddie's our friend," David spoke up, "and we're going to help him!"

"If he's a runaway I won't!" Two-tooth Clarabella's hands were on her hips. Even in the dark you could see her face harden.

"Is your momma's friend, Miss Annie Drummond, a runaway?" Ida shot the question at Two-tooth. Irish Mabel spun around and started toward the alley beside Rag-Picker Judson's place at once.

"Annie Drummond ain't no runaway," Irish Mabel roared back. Ida, David and me followed her. A half-second later so did Two-tooth. Rag-Picker Judson's Saloon was long and narrow. Irish Mabel whispered for all of us to move quietly. From what she knew the back half of the building was a storage area and beyond it a small yard. The alley reeked of garbage and foul odors, but we were forced to move slowly lest we be discovered. At one point, before we reached the end, Two-tooth thought she was going to faint from the smell, but Ida whispered that if she fell, whatever was on the ground would cover her clothes. The thought of smelling worse than we did seemed to keep Two-tooth upright. When we reached the end of the alley Irish Mabel signaled us to stop. She crouched and slowly peeped around the corner of the building, then held up two fingers.

"One young, one older," Irish Mabel said.

"How are we gonna get pass two guards?" Ida whispered.

"I don't like it," Two-tooth intoned. "Why would anybody have to guard folks that ain't runways or fugitives?"

"You ain't never heard of shanghaiing?" She was getting on my nerves. A man's freedom was at stake.

"Shhh!" It was Ida. "You want to get us caught?"

"I got an idea," Irish Mabel said. "Come on Ida!"

The two girls stepped into the dim light around the corner of the building like a pair of precision dancers.

■ ■ ■

"What are you two beauties, doin' out at night, eh?"

The voices surprised Freddie, because at the same time he heard one of the guards speak to what he thought were two women outside, Smoke managed to free himself from his shackles. With the help of a

rusty nail he began to free everyone. First Freddie, then
Annie and the others.

■ ■ ■

"We came to see what the runaways looked like,"
Irish Mabel said. David and me moved to the edge of
the alley. Ida and Irish Mabel marched forward, just
outside the reach of the two men. Two-tooth Clarabella
hung back. She was on edge, and mildly frightened.

"They're locked inside, *pretty*," the young one said,
"and I'll let you see 'em if I can look up your skirt!"

Irish Mabel kicked up her right leg and smiled. "I'll
think about it," she said.

"What about you, you colored wench?" The older
man pointed to Ida and took a mini-step toward her.

■ ■ ■

*"These locks were made by Plimington Brothers on
Centre Street," Smoke laughed. "It was the first place
I apprenticed when I reached New York!"*

*The man named Hoggard wanted to break out at
once, but Smoke slowed him down. There was something familiar about him, but I wasn't sure what. He
could have been a fellow I had seen in Pete Williams',
Almacks Saloon.*

*"All of us have to get away, Mr. Hoggard, and not be
re-caught," he said. "Besides, the doors are bolted from*

the outside! If we escape near dawn, when they come to take us to court, the light will give us cover—Nash and Snatch can't work in the daylight—especially aroun' here, where everybody knows we ain't runaways!"

Annie pointed at me. "Except for him!" I was speechless but in that moment I tightened my fists ready to fight. To my surprise, I heard David.

"Leave my sister alone," David shouted, stepping into the shadows slightly beyond the glow of the light. It was a perfect move and pulled the two men off guard, leaving a straight path to the door and the bolt that locked it.

"I know that voice," Smoke said.

Freddie heard one of the guards curse. "You little cockroach! I'll beat the living crap outta yah!"

The older man lunged toward David, and as soon as he moved, I ran to the door and slid the bolt out of the lock.

At the sound of the bolt, Hoggard charged the door, at once crashing into the yard behind the building and knocking the older man down. The rest of us followed him out as the young man started to holler.

■ ■ ■

We were surprised to see Smoke, who grabbed the young man and shoved him against a wall so hard, he slid to the ground unconscious. When he turned toward the old man, he dropped his truncheon and cowered in a corner of the yard, begging Smoke not to hit him. Out the corner of my eye, I saw Ida toss something at the old man. It hit him in the face just as Freddie came toward us, smiling. He thanked David and me, and we introduced him to the Brewery Witches. Freddie thanked them and shook their hands. Irish Mabel proudly told him, chest out; "It was my idea to set all of you *coloreds* free!" Two-tooth Clarabella took the praise but told Smoke she'd appreciate it if he didn't tell *anybody* she had anything to do with getting them out. He promised her he wouldn't tell anyone. Ida quietly said "you're welcome," to Freddie, then started out of the alley, her head down.

"Hey, we're not out of this mess yet, everybody."

"Why not?" It was Mr. Hoggard who was halfway down the alley, a cane under his arm. Ida stopped as well.

"We still have to get back to the Old Brewery," Smoke said, "and before we do, I'd like to get my hands on Snatch, and unmask him so Mr. Ruggles and the Committee of Vigilance can expose him before everybody!"

"I think I got a good look at him in the Old Brewery," said Freddie.

"You did?" It was Mr. Hoggard.

Freddie nodded. "I know he's a colored man, 'bout your height—younger than you."

"Well, you hunt him if you want, Sir, but I want to get back to my family," Hoggard spoke as he spun around and rushed out of the alley ahead of Ida.

"Ida, are you going home?" I asked. She didn't answer. By the time we were on Leonard Street, Irish Mabel and Two-tooth Clarabella had caught up to her and the three of them were headed back to the Old Brewery.

The Three Brewery Witches, I thought. *An appropriate name for them.*

Mr. Hoggard had disappeared.

■ ■ ■

David asked, "Are you going to be alright, Freddie?"

"He can stay with me until it's safe," said Smoke. "How are you two getting home?"

David and me looked at each other, then at Smoke and Freddie.

"I think we're in trouble, Mr. Smoke," I said.

"I know we are," added David grimly.

"I'll tell you what, I'll take you home," Smoke spoke optimistically, "your daddy, Mr. Little, has always been an understanding man, and I'll tell him exactly what happened, and how if it hadn't been for you two, six of us would have been on a boat, on our way down South to slavery! How's that?"

"Thanks, Mr. Smoke," David reached for his hand and shook it. So did I but I asked, "Do you need to tell him all of it?" Smoke smiled. We were both breathing easier as Freddie began to tell us what had happened to him as we started toward home. But life has a way of upending the best of our hopes. We weren't a half-block from our home when I heard a loud, angry voice.

"Charles and David Little, where in the h— have you been?"

Dad had cursed. Something he never did! He was storming up Leonard Street, growling. If I didn't know anything else, I was certain, if David and me weren't dead, we could bet we'd soon wish we were, because our dad was sure to kill us.

CHAPTER SEVEN

MOTHER WAS IN TEARS ONCE she saw us and though Dad was furious, he withheld his rage until he marched us to our room and closed the door. His belt came off so fast, I nearly missed his yanking it from his pants. It seemed to me it suddenly appeared in the air above us out of nowhere. Like a long, flying, leather snake whose tail could move independently of its head, the edge of the belt came down on David and me hard and fast enough for both of us to nearly howl at once. Though he only struck us once I heard David yell *two* times! I could be wrong. I was yelling so loud from my own pain I can't be sure I heard anything correctly. But something strange was happening to Dad. In the middle of his second swing, he stopped suddenly.

"If you *ever* do anything like that again—!" His voice got caught in his throat. Was he crying? Even though I was face down on the bed holding my backside, it sounded like he was crying. I didn't dare turn around, though David almost did, before he was stopped, when Dad told him not to move. There was a moment of quiet. Dad seemed to catch his breath before he spoke again.

"Don't you ever! Your mother and I thought we had lost you!" His voice was shaking and then, suddenly it turned angry again. "You mean everything to us! Do you understand that? Huh? *Huh?*"

"Yyeess, Ddaadddyy," we almost said that at the same time. The room was quiet for a moment. We heard him cross to the door and slam it shut behind him. I caught our mother ask him if we were alright.

"They're alright, but they smell awful! And, I tanned 'em, Alice, but it hurt me more than it did them!"

What? Hurt him more than it hurt us? My backside is stinging, not his!

"Why do they always say that," David asked, turning over. It was hard to lay on our backs so we faced each other on our sides.

I shrugged, wiping away tears. "They're adults, that's why! Sometimes D, nothing they say makes any sense!"

It was one of the few times David and me agreed with each other. Mother came in soon after and we both got baths. David went to sleep first. It had been a long night. Outside, dawn was fighting its way back into Five Points, and I thought about Dirty...*it's hard to call her just plain Ida*—and how she looked when she walked away from us. She seemed so gloomy! And I'm not saying I was beginning to *like* her, the way you like a girlfriend, or anything like that! Nothing of the sort. I just wondered where she'd go, since she didn't feel she had a mother—and if she'd be alright. I laid awake for awhile remembering what happened once we saw Dad.

Neither Smoke nor Freddie said anything that would implicate David and me in their rescue from the slave catchers. Yet nothing seemed to calm our dad's anger. Before they departed, Smoke asked my dad to tell Mr. Ruggles he wanted to see him. Still angry, my dad thanked them for protecting us and promised Smoke he would tell Mr. Ruggles.

■ ■ ■

The news on Little Water Street that morning was filled with stories about the raid on the Old Brewery and how it was foiled by three little girls who called themselves The Brewery Witches. Even a few of the do nothing Magus took some credit for chasing the slave catchers. David was livid, but we couldn't tell anyone the truth.

"Or call any attention to ourselves," I told him. "If we do, they'll ask us why we did it, and where would Freddie be then?" I think we were both convinced, though we didn't say it to each other, that Freddie was obviously a runaway slave. The news didn't stop Daniel Nash and his Black-Birders from parading Grandpa Jackson, Vincent the Gash, and several others from the court house, with a squad of Watchmen to a ship waiting on the East River. They didn't dare walk them past Little Water Street or the Old Brewery. Once we awakened, I showed Dad the canvas bag I'd fished out of the water the day before. Surprised, he examined the belt and the sheet of paper, showed them to our mother and rushed David and me to get dressed.

"We've got to take these to the Cullen family," he said.

Sleepy and yawning, we followed Dad out of the house and across Cow Bay. Yep, sleep or no sleep, David and me went back to work. Dad had two chimneys to sweep—a house on Centre Street near the Tombs Prison and one on Bayard Street close to Mulberry Street. But he headed in the opposite direction, toward Chatham Street, where the Cullen family lived. When we reached their tenement, there were many Cullen family members and friends milling around. The loss of a child to kidnappers and slave catchers in Five Points was considered nearly as terrible as if they had died.

"Wait by the door, boys."

Dad gave us his bucket of tools and went inside, climbing the stairs to the third floor where Mrs. Cullen and her sister, Mrs. Rudolph, lived. Almost at once we heard a loud, anguished cry coming from the opened window of the third-floor flat. People around us looked up. Mrs. Cullen had rushed to the window and was leaning dangerously over its edge, sobbing and screaming, when we saw Dad yank her back into the room. It was then, when David and me and the crowd were relieved that Mrs. Cullen hadn't jumped, that I realized

we were being followed or watched. Sitting on the steps
of a building across the street, pretending to be minding
his own business, was Pickles the Killer who didn't look
up until our dad came downstairs. Dad was downcast
when he picked up his bucket.

A man in the crowd asked him, "How is she,
Little?"

"Not good, Uncle Larry. Not good."

We headed to the first job in silence. David and me
always carried Dad's ladder and several brooms to the
jobs. Dad would carry the bucket with heavy tools, but
this day he wanted to carry everything.

"You two just stay in front of me—out where I
can see you!"

When we left the first job, I could swear I saw
Pickles duck behind the wall of the last house on the
corner of Leonard Street, and as we turned east onto
Franklin Street, the Tease greeted us. He was leaning
against a wall near the police station.

"Hello, Mr. Little," he said, smiling. "And how are
you two smart sons of a hard-working father? That's
dangerous work you doin', Mr. Little. A fella could fall
off a roof and hurt hisself real bad!"

"How would you know what could happen to
anyone who has a *job,* when you've never had one,
Sir," our dad said.

The Tease made a nasty face once Dad had passed
him, but he didn't say anything else. I looked back at
him, and he swung his arm up in the air quickly, while
snapping his fist shut, in a gesture that suggested he

would catch us like flies, in his hand. He frightened me so much I spent the rest of our workday looking over my shoulder for him or Pickles. Dad noticed.

"Why are you so jumpy, Charlie," he asked, as we headed back to Little Water Street. "You've been looking behind yourself all day, son!"

I shrugged and said; "Nothing's wrong."

Suddenly Dad looked up and saw Mr. Ruggles crossing Orange Street in our direction. He waved and Mr. Ruggles hurried forward.

"On your way home?"

Mr. Ruggles nodded. "Just left Reverends Caufield and Cornish. We tried to persuade Riker to hold Grandpa Jackson and the Gash over for a hearing tomorrow—it would've given us time to get them set free, but he refused. Said a man named Hoggard, who we saw leaving the court, knew both of them in Alabama and swore they were runaways."

David and me looked at each other.

"Mr. Ruggles, Sir, was Mr. Hoggard an old man with a beard?" David blurted out the question.

"Yes! Do you boys know him? I'd never seen the man before. There's no one in these parts named Hoggard—not in the Old Brewery or the surrounding streets."

Dad glared at me. "How do you know about this man?"

Why look at me? Did I say anything about Mr. Hoggard?

120

"He was one of the people we saw with Smoke last night," David answered.

"He was caught in the raid?" Mr. Ruggles was puzzled.

David and me both shrugged. Now wasn't the time to start describing what had happened. Dad's expression was beginning to look pretty grim, as though he was remembering how angry he had been last night.

"By the way, Smoke wants to see you, Ruggles."

Mr. Ruggles nodded his head, but he was deep in thought.

"I've got to get home to my supper," Dad said, and started away. Mr. Ruggles stopped him.

"Can I ask your boys another question, Robert?" Dad nodded, as Mr. Ruggles looked down at the two of us.

"Did either of you notice anything unusual about Mr. Hoggard?"

I searched my memory, but could think of nothing out of the ordinary about the man.

"His beard wasn't real," David said.

"Yes it was," I argued.

"No it wasn't," he defended. "He moved it when he started out of the alley—from here," David touched the bottom of his jaw on the left side, "to here!" He raised his finger maybe a half inch.

How could he have seen that? The alley was dark! Plus, Dad is looking suspiciously at him and me!

"He wasn't old either," David finished.

121

"You sure?" Mr. Ruggles bent forward.

David nodded. "I'm sure."

"How do you know?"

"He only pretended to need his cane. When he walked out of the alley behind Dirty Ida, it was under his arm."

There you go! He just told the whole thing! Good grief!

Mr. Ruggles straightened. "When we saw him this morning, he was using it—in fact he needed help to walk!"

"Could Hoggard be Snatch?" Dad asked.

"Wish I knew," Mr. Ruggles spoke and started away. "We've got to expose this person, Robert. He's a danger to us all! Thank you, boys!" Mr. Ruggles continued up Orange Street and we headed home. Suddenly, we heard someone behind us shout.

"You're next Mister Ruggles!" It was several Black-Birders leaning on the corner of Orange and Franklin Streets. "We've got a lovely boat in the East River just waitin' for troublemakers like you and your Committee, to take a nice sunny trip down South! Can't wait to see you shackled!"

Without replying, Mr. Ruggles kept walking west on Franklin Street. As we grew closer to Little Water Street we caught a glimpse of Irish Mabel and Two-tooth Clarabella running toward Mulberry Street, where they were sweeping the crossings for uptown swells. They didn't see David and me, but I wondered why Ida wasn't with them. Could she have really run away? I realized as we started up the stairs to our rooms, I intended to find out—and maybe—a pretty big *maybe,* find out who Mr. Hoggard really was.

"How is it you two know so much about this Hoggard?" It was Dad and we had no choice but to tell him the truth.

■ ■ ■

For the next several days, against our mother's wishes, we were not even permitted to go to school. Dad was so angry with us he would barely speak to us at supper, and as soon as the sun went down, we were ordered to bed. One morning however, after nearly seven days of what David and me called our captivity, our presence was requested at the home of Mr. Ruggles. When Mother showed the note to our dad, he grumbled, but finally gave in to her soft-spoken request to allow us to go.

"After all, it's a wedding, Robert," we heard her say, "and we haven't enjoyed many afternoons lately."

David and me were so happy we almost revealed that we had been listening at the door. The following day, Mother soaked our clothes while David and me scrubbed off the chimney soot that clung to us no matter how often or how hard we washed. When the time came to leave, we looked as though we were going to church. Trimmer Spurts saw us leaving and thought we were heading to a burial. Removing his ever-present hat, he nodded solemnly to Dad.

"Tell whoever it *is*'s family, I mourn wit 'em, Mr. Little. I mourn wit' 'em!"

Dad just shook his head as we started down the stairs.

■ ■ ■

Mr. Ruggles lived in a house at #67 Lispenard Street, where he had a bookstore, library, small press and sometimes held meetings of the Committee of Vigilance. It was outside of Five Points but close enough for Mr. Ruggles to be involved in everything related to the kidnapping of freemen, women and children. But as we walked up Centre Street, my hand began to itch. I felt we were being watched or followed. Sure enough, when we crossed the intersection at the corner of Lispenard and Church Streets, David nudged me and gestured. When I glanced behind us, smiling at the corner, Pickles and Bullets Lanham both waved like street-bound vultures. I admit, they had me worried.

Someone must want to frighten us so bad, we'll let down our guard, I thought. We reached Mr. Ruggles' house. The front windows were covered over so no one outside could see in and we could not see out. The rear windows were open however, and Smoke's sister Mariah led us to the back of the house, where Freddie greeted us and our parents, then introduced us to a free woman from Baltimore.

"I wanted to thank you two for all you did for me," Freddie said, "and make sure you met my wife-to-be!"

"Why are you getting married," David asked perturbed.

My Dad cleared his throat as Smoke, Mr. Ruggles, an older man named Stewart and several others laughed. I recognized Reverends Pennington,†† Evans and Caufield in the room.

"It's a question well directed," Rev. Caufield added. "Why does anyone marry in these dangerous times?"

David turned and looked at Reverend Caufield and for a second I could swear he froze.

"To start a family and build a better life, *Reverend*," our mother shot back at Reverend Caufield. It was clear he had annoyed her as well as Smoke's sister Mariah who looked daggers at the man.

"Could we begin the service," Rev. Pennington interjected, cracking the tension. Our Dad and Mr. Ruggles breathed simultaneous sighs of relief as Freddie and his bride-to-be moved together and Reverend Pennington opened his Bible.

David and me had never been to a wedding before Freddie's. What seemed strange to both of us, was how little each person said, for something that grown ups made such a fuss over. Freddie said, "I do," followed rather hurriedly by, "I do," from his bride, and that was that. Almost immediately Freddie and his wife were led into a room in the rear where for a short while we enjoyed cakes and lemonade. It was the last time we'd see Freddie for many years. Mr. Ruggles then asked everyone if we would forego any more celebration and leave at once.

"The newlyweds would like some private time together," he said, "and it's nearly dusk and I'd like everyone to reach home safely."

He explained that during the previous two days three free people, out after dark, had gone missing. "Two sailors and a young girl."

I immediately thought of Dirty Ida.

"Is the girl Ida Washington, Mr. Ruggles?"

"Noo! After the raid on the Old Brewery, poor Mrs. Washington took her Ida to the Colored Orphan Asylum," he said.[1]

"But Dirty Ida's—ah, Ida's not an orphan," David offered.

"She's considered a *half-orphan*," Mr. Ruggles answered. "A mother but no father."

I breathed a sigh of relief, but my mother, Dad and David were looking at me with puzzled expressions. Well, not David. He had a smirk on his face as my Dad led us out of Mr. Ruggles' house and down Lispenard Street.

I guess you could say, "That was that." Freddie was married, safe, and David and me would find out later that he and his wife left New York that evening and went to New England. So, everything *seemed* fine.

"Do you want to tell us about Ida Washington, *Charles*," Mother asked. She was teasing.

"No," I replied.

"He likes her," David laughed.

"I do not!" I wanted to toss him in front of an on-coming carriage, but Reverend Caufield called us from behind and distracted me. He was a man around my

Dad's age—or slightly older—Dad didn't have any gray hair, while Reverend Caufield's temples were graying.

"Would you mind if I walk with you?" Rev. Caufield joined us in stride, smiling down at David and me. "I hope you weren't offended by what I said, Mrs. Little."

"Not at all Reverend, men often say things without thinking," Mother said. Our Dad cleared his throat. "How is Mrs. Caufield?"

"I'm afraid my wife won't be with us for awhile. Her sister was taken sick and she returned to Boston to care for her. I was thinking, if your boys would like to visit the Colored Orphan Asylum and see their friend—what was her name?"

"Ida," I said.

"Yes. Ida! I'd be happy to take them. I go there once a week and deliver a gospel message."

"These two aren't going *anywhere* for some time to come," Dad said.

"Sorry! I didn't mean to—!"

"You didn't."

We reached Leonard Street and Reverend Caufield stopped.

"I'm afraid I must leave you. There's a family in need on Thomas Street and I promised I'd visit to console the sick widow and her children." He tipped his hat to my mother and took his leave, hurrying down Church Street.

"Hmph! Never heard of a Preacher who can't seem to find a church!" Mother was skeptical. "I'd be willing to wager his wife was glad to leave!"

When we reached home, Trimmer Spurts yelled at us from his window. "How was the *burial,* Mr. Little? Dry and lively, or wet and sad?"

As we started up the stairs, he came out of his room and stood beside the bannister on the first floor.

"Neither," Dad said. "We went to a wedding."

"Now that's something," Trimmer said. "By the way, 'been a couple vermin watchin' this tenement we livin' in for several days. That rat, Tease and that Black-Birdie, Bullets. You know why?"

Dad shook his head, no, and we entered our rooms.

Before we went to bed, I overheard Mother asking Dad to reduce our punishment, but he refused.

"They have to be taught a lesson, Alice! In times like these children as well as adults have to be vigilant! I'll never forget the look on Daisy Cullen's face when I showed her Buster's belt in that bag the boy's fished outta the water! Never!"

David and me laid in bed silent for a long time staring at the ceiling.

"You think we'll ever be off punishment, Charlie?"

"Maybe—in a hundred years," I said depressed.

"It'll probably be a thousand," David turned over. He was sleepy. "Charlie, Reverend Caufield is Mr. Hoggard."

I sat up! "Are you sure?" David nodded. "How do you know?"

"They're both wearing the same pair of shoes," he said and fell asleep.

I tried to go to sleep, but it was well after midnight before I drifted off. Might Reverend Caufield, in addition to being Mr. Hoggard, also be, Snatch?

■　■　■

From September to Christmas is the busiest time of the year for the chimney sweep profession. The next four days David and me barely had time to eat, much less talk! We would come home exhausted and after eating supper go right to bed. Then, Dad would get us up at six, and as soon as we dressed, we'd be out the door again carrying ladder, brushes and lunch pails. We managed to eat only when Dad decided we could take a breather, but he never let us out of his sight. We weren't permitted to go fishing, to the green-grocer—*anywhere,* without Dad or Mother. When the four days threatened to stretch into five and perhaps a week in which we might not *even* be allowed to attend *Sunday* school, David and me decided we had to say something.

"Dad, why can't we do anythin' by ourselves anymore," David asked. We were eating supper.

"We can't go fishing—nowhere, without you or Mother," I added.

Dad leaned back in his chair and glared at both of us. "You two are lucky I don't tie you up and feed you bread and water!"

"Robert, you promised me," Mother spoke gently, interrupting him. For a moment Dad rose and just turned away from her. When he faced us again his voice was softer and his expression more troubled.

"Do you remember what mother told you about slavery?" We both nodded. "Slipping from your room was bad enough, but then I find out you two were actively involved in helping a fugitive escape—you could have been arrested and sent to prison—and we would not have been able to do anything to prevent it! Did you think about that?"

"But you told us to help runaways," I said. "You said all people need to be free!"

"I know," he said it and was quiet for a moment. "That's why we have a Vigilance Committee—some things are better left to older people, son—you two will be safer in a school. Leave the helping runaways to us, alright?"

Safer in a school?

"But nobody caught *us*, and we're safe now, Dad," David said smiling. His smile however, was met with a face that turned to stone.

"You'll be safer with—supervision!"

"Can't we go—go to school by ourselves anymore?" The words were not exactly a question. It seemed to be what he meant. Afterall, we always went to school together or with friends. If we were only safe with supervision—I don't need to say the obvious.

"Are you going to give us to the Colored Orphan Asylum?" David was about to cry.

Dad looked at mother. Mother looked at Dad.

"No! Not at all," Mother said, standing. "*That,* we are not going to do!"

"But, I thought we—," Dad sputtered something. He seemed surprised as Mother walked to the window and looked down at the alley beside Reverend Caufield's place. "They would be safe, Alice!"

"How do you know?" Mother turned around glancing at David and me. She was on the verge of crying. "Just suppose the Birders raided the Asylum and stole them from there—what then, Robert? This Snatch is everywhere!"

I couldn't believe it! Our parents were *actually considering* putting David and me in the Colored Orphan Asylum! *To protect us?*

What kind of trash is that?

Right then and there I decided, if it was the last thing I ever did in life, I would unmask Snatch and do everything I could to put the New York Kidnapping Club out of business.

So help me God!

■ ■ ■

David and me were put to bed early that night but whatever our Mother and Dad said to each other, the following day, Dad said we could go back to school. However, he gave David and me whistles.

"Put these around your necks and wherever you are," he said, "if you are in any danger, blow them three times—as loud as you can—over and over, and I promise you, help will be on the way."

They were short, round, gray metal things, tied to a soft leather cord, and the harder you blew them, the louder they sounded. Just wearing them made David and me feel safer. And bigger! They were the same whistles members of the Committee of Vigilance carried. Dad would tell us later that we didn't have the whistles before because Mr. Ruggles had to order them from Massachusetts. Mother gave us our morning meal and a few final instructions.

"Remember, blow three times!"

"Fast or slow," David asked.

"Fast," she said, "but make sure each blast is distinct, and heard! You're all we have, don't let anything happen to you. Charles, no matter what, protect your brother! And David, the same goes for you!"

We both said we would, and had learned our lesson. I fingered my whistle as we left the house. We never told Dad what David uncovered about Mr. Hoggard and Reverend Caufield. We should have, but sometimes, when all you can think about is being freed from punishment, important things can be forgotten. I remembered though as soon as David and me headed toward Cow Bay on our way to school, and I realized the Tease and Dicky the Map were stalking us. Two-tooth Clarabella told us about the Map. He had a reputation for knowing every tunnel, back alley, sewer and escape route in Five Points and was pretty high-up among the Black-Birders.

The Free Colored School had moved from William Street to Laurens Street the previous year. While William Street was little more than six blocks away from our rooms, Laurens was more than double that distance, though closer to Mr. Ruggles' house on Lispenard Street. David and me ran most of the way. We knew the Tease and Dicky the Map would be behind us, but if they looked like they were chasing us, people in the neighborhood who knew us would start shouting questions at them—something they couldn't afford. Everyone in Five Points knew David and me were not runaways or fugitive slaves.

It was good to be back in school. Most of our friends had heard about the raid on the Old Brewery and we spent most of our mid-morning recess describing how we escaped Pickles and Snatch. We also told our buddies about the Tease and Dicky the Map who were both lounging around a corner across the street from the school, and we made secret plans for them when school dismissed. It wasn't until we were back in the classroom that I realized I hadn't mentioned Ida and what she had done. I felt bad about it and promised myself not to forget her again. After recess our teacher, Ole'-Hit-You-With-A-Switch Moses Bowman, came into the classroom with the Reverends Caufield and Evans. David and me glanced at each other even though we were on different sides of the room.

"Class, we have guests," Ole'-Hit-You-With-A-Switch said, "and they've come to take us to see the

Colored Orphan Asylum on Twelfth Street and Sixth Avenue."

"Are the girls goin' wit us?" a classmate had raised his hand and asked. Reverend Evans smiled and shook his head. "Not today boys, we've only got two wagons and just enough space for most of you. The girls will go next week."

"Does everybody have to go?" David asked.

Ole'-Hit-You-With-A-Switch spoke at once, glancing at Reverend Caufield. "Not everyone, but you and your brother haven't been in school for awhile, Mister Little. Our visit today will be part of a test you will take tomorrow." He smiled at David then turned to me. His cold stare made me shudder.

Could Ole'-Hit-You-With-A-Switch, be Snatch?

Most of us boys were loaded into two wagons. David and the younger boys piled onto the first one, me and the older boys on the second. The draymen drove the flatbed wagons up Laurens Street to Washington Square, then up Fifth Avenue to Twelfth Street. Along the way we pointed at the fancy stores, pooh-poohed the expensive carriages and admired the well-dressed ladies and men. No one paid much attention to us, and when they did, they almost always glanced for a moment then quickly turned away. It was a hot day. By the time we reached the Colored Orphan Asylum most of us were thirsty and hungry. So me and a few friends of mine, when Ole'-Hit-You-With-A-Switch and the preachers turned their backs, began moaning and saying things like: "Water!" "I'm starving!" "Can't go any farther!" "Help!" Of course Ole'-Hit-You-With-A-Switch never knew which one of us said any of it. Annoyed, he marched us through the gates and into the courtyard that fronted Twelfth Street where a Quaker lady greeted us and told us she knew we were hungry—"And, we'll have something for you in a few minutes, boys!"

"Yayyyy!" Caps came off and most of us celebrated—at least I did, until I looked behind me across Twelfth Street, and saw Dicky the Map and the Tease. The Tease waved, then nudged Dicky the Map who nodded, broad smile across his face as he raised his hand and imitated *snatching* me out of the air, like he would a fly. I turned away, frightened, just as one of the teachers in the Colored Orphan Asylum marched a group of girls onto a porch and lined them up in three rows.

"Our choir has a song they want to sing to welcome you to our Orphan Asylum," the Quaker lady said.

She gestured to the woman who marched the girls out, and they all began singing, "My Country 'Tis Of Thee!" I didn't see Ida, but I began to move cautiously toward David. I wanted him to know we'd been followed all the way here by Snatch's lackeys. At first I tried to attract his attention, but he was playing some silly game with his friends and didn't see me. Ole'-Hit-You-With-A-Switch had seen him however, and was glaring at him so intensely, I thought the air around David and his friends would catch fire. When Ole'-Hit-You-With-A-Switch saw me, his gesture to move back was sharp and unmistakeable. I could only hope David had seen the Tease and Dicky the Map.

When the girls song was finished, Ole'-Hit-You-With-A-Switch led us boys through one verse of "Lord I Believe," and when I looked up, I saw Ida! I was so glad to see her I stopped singing! She was dressed in a uniform and apron staring down at the courtyard sadly from one of the second floor windows. I tried to wave but she didn't see me. I decided then and there that if an opportunity presented itself, I'd try to see her.

At the end of our song, the Quaker lady led us up the courtyard steps, past the girls, and into the Colored Orphan Asylum where bedlam broke out. In a large alcove, the Quaker ladies who ran the asylum set up two tables covered with food. When my classmates saw it, they rushed the tables and began pushing and shoving one another in an effort to get as much food as they could. Most of us had never seen that much food in one place, and knowing we could have any part of it drove many of my classmates into a frenzy. Ole'-Hit-You-With-A-Switch didn't know what to do. At first he started shouting: "Boys! Boys, where are your manners? Boys!"

Reverend Evans joined in when several of my classmates started throwing bread at one another.

"Gentlemen! This is not Five Points! In genteel surroundings, one must behave in genteel ways!"

My classmates ignored him. It was then that I began snaking my way toward David and a stairway that seemed to lead to the second floor. No one was paying any attention to me. The preachers and the

Quaker ladies were occupied with my classmates and the girls who came in from the courtyard to watch them. David got hit on the shoulder with an apple just before I reached him. Angered, he started to throw it back when I grabbed his arm.

"Don't throw it," I said. "Ida's upstairs; we've got to help her!"

I was already moving toward the staircase when he asked, "Why?"

"She's not an orphan is she?" was the best reason I could give. It seemed to make sense to him because he followed me up the stairs to the second floor, then along a hallway to the window where I saw her brooding. She wasn't there, so I started whispering her name.

"Ida? Ida? It's David and me! Where are you?"

I had turned in every direction when David tapped me on the shoulder and pointed to a chest beside the wall. Ida peeped out.

"What the (so-and-so) are you doing here, Ringworm." Leave it to Ida to be rude to the people who came to rescue her.

"My name is *Charles* and we came to get you out of here, Ida!"

"I'm not going any (so-and-so) where!"

"Why? You're not an orphan," David said.

"It's none of your business!"

"It's about your mother isn't it," I asked her point blank.

"I said, it's none of your (so-and-so) business!" She was about to cry, something I had never seen her do.

"Do you want to stay here, in this dark place, dressed in that uniform and never see your friends again?"

"Our mother can help you," David said.

"Can she help *you?*" The voice was menacing and belonged to Reverend Caufield who stepped out from the shadows, laughing. "We've been looking for your little friend here, and now it looks like we found all of you!"

"We're not afraid of you," I said, "our teacher Mr. Bowman, will be looking for us!"

"Will he? I think not—take a look out the window. After all that disturbance, Mr. Bowman felt it would be prudent to take you Five Point vermin back where you belong!"

David looked out the window. "They're leaving, Charlie!" I joined him. Below us the two wagons were pulling away from the gate and heading east on Twelfth Street. My heart sank.

"I told Mr. Bowman I'd gather you up—but, I didn't think I could find you," Reverend Caufield said, smiling triumphantly. "Somehow you *two*—and now *three,* slipped by me and wound up in the hands of slave catchers!"

He started laughing again when suddenly, Ida gave him a swift kick in his shin. He howled like an injured goat and grabbed his leg. The three of us started running immediately. Down the stairs, through the alcove, past the girls and out the front door into the courtyard. We rushed the gate just as one of the Quaker ladies was about to close it. Seeing Ida run past her into Twelfth

Street surprised the Quaker lady so much she failed to speak until we were running toward Fifth Avenue and the wagons.

"Ida Washington! You come back here at once!"

Her astonishment attracted the attention of the Tease and Dicky the Map. For a moment they didn't know what to do until they heard Reverend Caufield shouting at them.

"Get after them! After them!" He was in the window waving his arms.

We were running so fast it felt as though we were flying. By the time we reached Fifth Avenue, the wagons had reached Tenth Street but I had an idea. If we jumped on the wagons so close to the Colored Orphan Asylum, they might stop or turn around to take Ida back. We had to get far enough away from the asylum so returning her would be a major inconvenience for Ole'-Hit-You-With-A-Switch and Reverend Evans. So I decided to turn at Eleventh Street and run back to Sixth Avenue.

"What are you doing?" Ida yelled. "Don't you want to catch the wagons?"

We stopped for a moment to catch our breath.

"Yep! But further down—maybe even avoid them."

"We can't outrun the Tease!" David was panting.

"We can't, but a carriage can!"

Ida's eyes lit up. "Let's go!"

We started running again just as I saw the Tease and Dicky the Map turn onto Eleventh Street. All we had to do was reach Sixth Avenue and hop on the back of one of the light, swift-moving Hackneys or Landaus[2] and hope it wouldn't stop until the Tease or Dicky the Map got too tired to chase us. We were in luck. Sixth Avenue was crowded with carriages. "Meet you in Washington Square," Ida said.

Suddenly, she bolted into the avenue, chasing a fast-moving Landau pulled by two horses with only two people in its rear seat. The horses never slowed when Ida leaped onto the carriage.

David and me chased a Hackney racing toward Tenth Street. It stopped suddenly, however, and David and me nearly crashed into the rear of it. the Tease and Dicky the Map had split up. Dicky the Map chased Ida, while the Tease pursued David and me. The Tease was known as much for his speed as his skill as a pickpocket. And though David and me were running like rabbits, the chase was taking its toll on David. By the time we reached Ninth Street, David was showing signs of exhaustion. He was slowing down. He began to pant and run with his mouth open. I grabbed his hand and headed in the direction of a quick-moving Barouche carriage racing toward us. Just as it was about to pass us, I snatched David up, and said, "Grab the rear hitch and meet the wagons from school at Washington Square."

"What about you?"

"The Tease couldn't catch me if his life depended on it," I said. David stopped, as I watched the Barouche cross Eighth Street.

"We're brothers, Charlie, I'm not leaving you," he said, crossing his arms over his chest, that look of absolute stubbornness on his face. Sometimes little brothers can be a pain, and the Tease was nearly on top of us!

"Separate!"

David and me instantly ran in different directions, then circled behind the Tease and hooked up as we raced down Ninth Street back toward Fifth Avenue. It was a trick we had learned running from the Black-Birders. The Tease followed but he'd never catch us now. I even waved back at him, until I saw what was waiting for us on the corner of Fifth Avenue and Ninth. Who else but, Dicky the Map and Reverend Caufield, on either side of the quiet street, looking rather pleased and victorious. Now, I could have taken a chance and tried to dodge them, or tried a version of a trick I saw Irish Mabel use once in Paradise Square. Her trick involved crying. Mine? Well, I stopped and began shouting at Dicky the Map and the Tease.

"Our father's a freeman, Sir! Why are you two trying to sell us into slavery?"

"Yeah, we're free," David joined in immediately. "They're trying to kidnap us!"

We spun around and pleaded to people passing on the sidewalks.

"My father's a freeman, Miss! I was born in New York! These men are trying to kidnap me and my brother and sell us into slavery!"

"He's lyin'!" The Tease couldn't help but look guilty. "He's lyin' I tell yah!"

Down the street Reverend Caufield, who had started toward me, turned around and headed toward Sixth Avenue.

"They're thieves, these two are," Dicky the Map said. He and the Tease were closing in on David and me. I appealed to a well-dressed woman walking with her daughter.

"He works with the slave catchers! And he's trying to take us from our poor family, Miss! Our hardworking mother and father! I'm a freeman, born here in New York, Miss! New York!" The well-dressed woman frowned at the Tease then nudged her daughter away from the street.

Someone yelled, "Call a Watchman!"

At the sound of Watchman, the Tease slowed down.

"We'll be gone before they get here," Dicky the Map said, egging the Tease forward. People on the sidewalks were beginning to back away. Some were even trying to avoid looking in our direction. A shopkeeper came to his doorway and began laughing.

"You wanna bet they don't get away, Jackie?" he yelled up the street. David and me moved closer together.

"You gonna' let these kidnappers steal us?"

"That's your problem, Sunshine," the shopkeeper joked. He turned to Dicky the Map. "What did they steal?"

The kidding emboldened Dicky the Map and the Tease and just as they closed in I pulled on my whistle and blew three times as hard as I could. David started blowing his as well. One! Two! Three! Again and again! And suddenly, a window opened on the second floor of a cloth shop and a black woman stuck her head out and yelled down at the Tease and Dicky the Map.

"What you doin' to them boys, huh?"

The Tease stopped and looked up. At that moment, a black man carrying a sack set it down and yelled, "Leave them alone, Mister!" Dicky the Map was surprised at the man's tone but before he could say anything another woman cried out, "I know their momma! You leave them alone!"

"They're not runaways!"

The voices were coming from all directions. Up and down the street, Negroes who worked in the shops and on delivery wagons began to shout. Shop owners came out of their shops.

"Leave them alone, creeps!"

"You ain't gonna steal these two!"

"No Sir-ee! Not these two!"

"Git' on away from hea'!"

The Tease and Dicky the Map began to move away, slowly at first, uncertain whether or not to bow to this kind of pressure. But the pressure didn't stop. The owner of a flower shop came charging from his front door with a broom, threatening Dicky the Map. A woman, shopping with her mistress, grabbed the hand of her charge—a little girl, and started into the street.

"You betta not," she threatened.

That was it. The Tease turned and headed toward Fifth Avenue, lowering his head as he confronted the taunts of several black workmen and their foreman clearing trash from the street.

"This ain't your day, skinny!"

A few steps behind him Dicky the Map left sullenly.

"You skunks better get outta here—and quick!"

I turned to the people on the sidewalk, placed my hand over my heart and yelled, "Thank you!" then mouthed the words again as David and me strolled away. I made sure when we reached Fifth Avenue this time, the Tease, Dicky the Map or Reverend Caufield were nowhere in sight. We began walking cautiously down Fifth Avenue hoping we would see a dray loaded with barrels or boxes headed south. It would be easy to hop on, and whatever it was carrying could provide cover if the Tease, Dicky the Map or Reverend Caufield should be prowling. We only walked half a block when we saw what we needed: a four-horse wagon hauling furniture covered by a tarp. We hopped on one at a time so the horses wouldn't slow down too much. Most pedestrians were accustomed to seeing boys our age riding the tail ends of freight wagons so no one alerted the driver. The trip to Washington Square was surprisingly quick as it began to rain and the driver galloped his team most of the way. I saw Ida immediately. She was standing with Irish Mabel and one of the Magus at Amity Lane, one of the streets the Brewery Witches corner-swept. They were admiring her uniform until David and me approached.

"If I were you, I wouldn't stay too long in that uniform," I said.

"What do you know about it, Ringworm," Irish Mabel chided.

"I wasn't talking to you Irish Mabel," I shot back.

Before she could reply, Ida touched Irish Mabel's shoulder. She didn't say anything. Instead, she nodded to me, flashed a tiny smile and started walking toward Five Points followed by her friends.

What a secret person, I thought.

I realized then that Ida would always be a mystery to me, but one I wanted to know more about.

A few minutes later, the two wagons carrying the boys from school rolled into the square. Ole'-Hit-You-With-A-Switch was on board the first wagon while Rev. Evans was driving the second. Rev. Caufield, the Tease and Dicky the Map were nowhere in sight. We ducked behind a vegetable cart until the wagons passed, then started running toward Laurens Street and school. If we got there ahead of the wagons, I figured as long as we weren't hurt, things would be fine. I was right. Ole'-Hit-You-With-A-Switch scolded David and me for nearly five minutes and gave us extra homework, but he was relieved all the boys were safely back in school. But for the next several days Ole'-Hit-You-With-A-Switch hit every student involved in the mêlée at the Colored Orphan Asylum and gave a long lesson in *The Proper Etiquette for Students Visiting other Institutions.*

■ ■ ■

Before I forget! I had my thirteenth birthday five days after the mêlée. The next time we saw Freddie was several years later. He had changed his name to

Frederick Douglass, became a famous orator, and had written a book entitled, *Narrative of the Life of Frederick Douglass: An American Slave, Written by Himself with Related Documents*.

When David and me read the book, we didn't find one word about us and the things that happened that day and night in September, 1838. We were both happy about that. Our parents were among the first black people in Five Points to read the book after Freddie sent them a copy, and had he written anything about what we did that night, we would all have been in more trouble than you can imagine.[3] David and me thank Frederick Douglass to this day!

■ ■ ■

Ida came back to the girls' school and started living with her mother again, and David and me decided that the only way we could unmask Snatch was to look at every black man's shoes in Five Points. We were certain Snatch, Reverend Caufield and Mr. Hoggard were one and the same, but something rather peculiar happened. Reverend Caufield and Mr. Hoggard disappeared and have not been seen since! No one knows where they went, why or when. It simply happened that one day Reverend Caufield's flat was empty, and the next day an elderly gentleman with one arm calling himself Captain Bluefish Johnnie Williams occupied the place. He seemed a nice enough old man. He met our parents and seemed to take an interest in David and me. But we're pretty cautious these days, because Pickles the Killer, the Tease, Bobby Bullets Lanham and Dicky the Map are still in Five Points, and even though Captain Bluefish Johnnie Williams doesn't wear the same kind of shoes that Mr. Hoggard and Reverend Caufield wore—there's something about the man—something odd, and maybe even sinister. It's the way he looks at David and me sometimes whenever we see him on the street—and what he does! He'll walk toward us sometimes gesturing with his one good hand, in the same manner the Tease and Pickles did. It's as if he was about to catch us, and *snatch* us out of the air, the way he would a fly.

■ ■ ■

The End—for the moment!

AFTERWORD

NEARLY A HALF CENTURY AGO, I made a promise to my two sons, Charles III, and David Ira Fuller that I would write a story for them in which they would be the heroes of an adventure that would take place during a particular period of American history that not many African-Americans had spent a great deal of time researching. I chose the slave period in the North, and began researching what life was like in antebellum New York City before the Civil War and the Emancipation Proclamation. I even wrote an outline, and a first chapter, but because my life as a playwright was moving forward, I did not find the time or make time to keep that promise. The story you have just read, after forty years, is a promise fulfilled.

At the time, I wanted to dedicate the story to all the young people in my family, hoping that one, some, or all of them would find a reason to investigate our history in America further. Since then one can imagine the number of children who have been born into the ranks of Fullers and their marital extensions, but by dedicating this to a larger group my chances of having my hope realized is a lot closer now than in the past. So, I dedicate this story first to my parents Charles and Lillian Fuller, to my deceased wife, Miriam Fuller, and my second wife, Claire Prieto-Fuller, my son Charles III, his wife, Cathy and my grandsons, Charles IV and Gerald; my son David Ira, his wife Robin and my granddaughters, Meadow and Brooke; to Claire's son Ian Kamau Prieto-McTair; to my brother Walter, his wife Martine, and their sons, Walter Jr. and Cameron; to my deceased sister Mary and her children, Roland Shelton, and his daughter, Mason, Lillian Shelton, and Hollis Walker; to my sister Charlotte, her husband David and their children, Jessica Jahn and Daniel Jahn and his sons, Zack, Kamilo, and daughter Akara; to Miriam's mother Muriel Nesbitt, to Miriam's sister Beatrice Green and her children, Clarence, Ira, Cedric and his daughter, Shiniece and son Shamar, Muriel Pollard and her sons, Marcus, DeHaven and his daughter Skyllia Renee', Maurice and his daughter, Samiyh and son Maurice Jr.; to my uncle Walter Anderson and his children, Eric, Ernie, and his daughter Miranda, Robin and his son Edwin, Troy and his sons Troy, Jr., Aaron and Noah, and his daughters Nina, and April, Faith and her son Warren, Hannah and her daughter Chastity; to my aunt Lila Wescott and her children, Virginia Ann Barringer and her two sons, Matthew and Michael; Gerald, Lila, and Gary Smith and his son Jabril; to my aunt Elizabeth Dickerson and her children, Nathaniel, and his son Nate, and two daughters Angelica and Elizabeth, Evelyn, Monica and her two daughters Sabrina and Torrie, Elizabeth and her sons, Michael and Marcus; to my uncle Robert Fuller's children, Robert Jr. and his daughter Verlonda, Michael and his son Corey, Lance and his daughter Martika, Paula and her daughter Wynter; to my uncle William Fuller's children, Lisa and Lynne and her son, Kali; to my cousin Geraldine's children, Selma and her sons, Aaron and his daughters Arianna, Lawrence and Willy and his daughters Nicole, and Erica; to my cousin Marion and her children, Crystal, and her daughter Fathia, and son Nyquill, Shirley Rene', and her son Johfee and her daughter Faith, David, and his daughters Ashley and Asia, Ebony and her son Dayshon; to my cousin Marvalene and her children, Sherman and his sons, Germain and Morgan and his daughter, Charae, Geneva and her daughters, Lashia and Lashia's sons Dayon and Donovan, Kia and her daughter Gymia, Lawanda and her daughters, Giana and Ginia; to my cousin Frances, and her son Paris and granddaughter, LaBrida; to my cousin Frank and his son Vaughn; to my cousin Rachel Slaughter and her two children, Chelsea and Sadie, to my second cousin Marguerite Tiggs-Birt and her daughter, Amanda. To my second wife's family, her sister Gemma and her husband Alloy Mooking and their children, Carla and her daughter, Jade; Michael and his son Jackson and daughter India, Roger and his daughters Ruby and Isabel; Harold Prieto and his twins Ryan and Renee; Peter Prieto and his children Aaron, his daughters, Marsha and her children Mariah and Marlon; Raelene and her son, Jordan; Richard Prieto and his son Tarquin and daughter Yonelle; and for those who have become family, Evelyn Neal and her son Avatar Neal, Carl Gordon and his son Rufus and daughter Jasmine; Josette and her daughters, Trilana, Seani, and Nicole; Robert Magabet and his daughter Christine; Ivy Ziegler, and her daughter Amber and her son Elias, for Quinn, Monet and Monique; for Alberta and Jeanette Lites and her son Oscar, and his children, Isheen, Kiana, Kiera, Ciani, and Leonard; for Hadith and Brooklyn.

(and this list continues to grow)

Author's Note

THIS BOOK IS A WORK OF FICTION. The narrative, descriptions and dialogue are my invention. I am grateful to the authors of various scholarly works that I consulted for historical data regarding the time and place of the story and the lives of historical figures, including Frederick Douglass, who appear in this novel. My sources are given in the following endnotes and the bibliography.

—Charles Fuller

END NOTES

Notes to Chapter One

1. See, Burrows, Edwin G., and Mike Wallace, *Gotham: A History of New York City to 1898*. New York, 1999. A description of a group led by Black-Birders Elias Boudinot and Daniel D. Nash which called itself the New York Kidnapping Club notorious for snapping up victims. Straight-out kidnapping was illegal but if Black-Birders brought a captive before city recorder Riker and produced (paid) witnesses to swear he or she was a recent runaway, Riker usually authorized deportation. Pg. 561. *(n.b. smiling skull author's invention.)*

2. See Internet Sources: Ruggles, David. *"Emancipator"* November 2, 1836. Speech delivered recounting experience of Eliza Drummings, etc. Traitors Exposed. Ruggles mentions a slave, David Holliday in New York to betray...men, women and children to slavery. (Doc #01354). University of Detroit Mercy—Black Abolitionist Archive. *(n.b.* Snatch *is based on the idea of David Holliday.)*

3. Nearly every book about Five Points mentions the infamous Pete Williams, a black man who owned or

ran the saloon called Almacks but re-named Dickens Place once it was visited by Charles Dickens in 1842 and described in his *American Notes*. There is some discrepancy with regard to where Pete Williams saloon was. It is located on Orange Street in some histories and Slaughter House Point (James and Water Streets) in others. I have settled on the Orange Street location. See, Anbinder, Tyler, *Five Points: The 19th Century New York City Neighborhood that Invented Tap Dance, Stole Elections, and Became the World's Most Notorious Slum*. Pgs. 172–175, 198–199. See, Asbury, Herbert, *The Gangs of New York; An Informal History of the Underworld*. Pg. 60. See, Dickens, Charles, *American Notes for General Circulation. In Two Volumes*. Pg. 101. See, Foster, George G., *New York by Gas-Light*. Pgs. 130, 140–146. See, Harris, Leslie M., *In The Shadow Of Slavery: African Americans in New York City—1626–1863*. Pgs. 255–256. See, Ottley, Roi and William J. Weatherby, eds., *The Negro In New York: An Informal Social History, 1626–1940*. Pgs. 77–78. See, Robinson, Solon, *Hot Corn: Life Scenes In New York Illustrated: Including The Story Of Little Katy; Madalina, The Rag-Pickers Daughter; Wild Maggie, Etc*. Pg. 53.

4. See, Anbinder, Tyler, *Five Points: The 19th Century New York City Neighborhood that Invented Tap Dance, Stole Elections, and Became the World's Most Notorious Slum*. Pg. 14.

5. Watchmen was the name given to early police-like units that provided some law and order in New York. See, Burrows, Edwin G., and Mike Wallace, *Gotham: A History of New York City to 1898*. Pgs. 635–638.

6. Staggtown, a name given sections where blacks lived in New York. See Internet Sources: Osofsky,

Gilbert—Source: *The Journal of American History*, Vol. 55, No. 2 (Sep., 1968), pp. 243–255. The Enduring Ghetto Author(s): ? Published by: Organization of American Historians. (Pg. 244, footnote #2.)

7.	Chimney sweep was one of the jobs blacks could hold in antebellum New York. See, Harris, Leslie M., *In The Shadow Of Slavery: African Americans in New York City—1626–1863*. Pgs. 77, 78 (fig. 6), 80. See also, Anbinder, Tyler, *Five Points: The 19th Century New York City Neighborhood that Invented Tap Dance, Stole Elections, and Became the World's Most Notorious Slum*. Pg. 306.

8.	Dickens describes a pig he sees roaming the streets of Five Points. See, Dickens, Charles, *American Notes for General Circulation. In Two Volumes*. Pgs. 96–97.

9.	"Hot Corn, etc." quote from book. See, Robinson, Solon, *Hot Corn: Life Scenes In New York Illustrated: Including The Story Of Little Katy; Madalina, The Rag-Pickers Daughter; Wild Maggie, Etc*. Pgs. 13, 18–19, 44–45. See, Asbury, Herbert, *The Gangs of New York; An Informal History of the Underworld*. Pg. 7.

10.	For a discussion of the Five Points gangs and their origins, see Asbury, Herbert, *The Gangs of New York; An Informal History of the Underworld*. Pgs. 20–21. (*n.b. In this story the Dead Rabbits are always called Black-Birders.*)

Notes to Chapter Two

1.	*Pint-A-Blood Point* is a name the author created. Given the confusion regarding the location of Pete Williams' saloon it serves the needs of the story and the reader, to not add the name of Slaughter House Point to a location where it could not exist.

2. Gip. A cheat, swindler.
3. See, Asbury, Herbert, *The Gangs of New York; An Informal History of the Underworld.* Pg. 43. A complete description of Big Sue who was said to run a dive on what was called the Arch Block, which ran from Thompson to Sullivan Streets between Broome and Grand Streets. *(n.b. For purposes of this story she is the bouncer in Pete Williams' dive.)*
4. *Ibid. Hose.* Pg. 25. *(The customer having deposited his money on the bar, took an end of the hose in his mouth, and was entitled to all he could drink without breathing.)*
5. *Ibid.* Pg. 21. *(n.b. The author has added undershirts, plug hats and bowlers to the gang uniforms. It has been said that the Dead Rabbits [Black-Birders] would carry a dead rabbit impaled on a pike into battle.)*

Notes to Chapter Three

1. Panel thief. Defined as one who hid behind the panels in a room and once a prostitute's customer fell asleep, the panel thief would emerge from the space in the wall and rob him. See, Foster, George G., *New York by Gas-Light.* Pg. 96.
2. For a brief history of David Ruggles, see Internet Sources: Hodges, Graham Russel, (Spring/Summer) "David Ruggles: The Hazards Of Anti-Slavery Journalism," *Media Studies Journal, 14,* (2). *(n.b. Mr. Hodges' work is part of a larger biography of David Ruggles).* See: Harris, Leslie M., *In The Shadow Of Slavery: African Americans in New York City—1626–1863.* Pgs. 173, 206–215.
3. By 1834 the Manumission Society who operated the African Free Schools decided they would transfer the

two schools they operated to the public school system of New York City. They would no longer be called African Schools but Colored Free Schools since the public school system was segregated. By 1837 the transfer had been accomplished and the Colored Free School was moved from William Street to Laurens Street. See Internet Sources: Palmer, A. Emerson, M.A., *The New York Public School: Being a History of Free Education in the City of New York*. New York, 1905. *Google Books*. Chapter XI: Schools of the Manumission Society Transferred. Pgs. 88–89. See also: Harris, Leslie M., *In The Shadow Of Slavery: African Americans in New York City—1626–1863*. Pg. 144.

Notes to Chapter Four

1. For information on crossing-sweepers, see: Foster, George G., *New York by Gas-Light*. Pg. 100.
2. Nearly every book about Five Points mentions or has a description of Cow Bay. A notorious cul-de-sac at the end of Little Water Street, it was noted for its crime and inter-racial relationships, as well as a place where Negroes fought battles with Watchmen (police). It also housed a number of Blind pigs, or speakeasies—Jacob's Ladder, Gates of Hell and Brick Bat Mansion being the most notorious. See: Anbinder, Tyler, *Five Points: The 19th Century New York City Neighborhood that Invented Tap Dance, Stole Elections, and Became the World's Most Notorious Slum*. Pgs. 91–93. See also: Asbury, Herbert. *The Gangs of New York; An Informal History of the Underworld*. Pgs. 11–12. Foster, George G., *New York by Gas-Light*. Pgs. 125–126. Burrows, Edwin G., and Mike Wallace, *Gotham: A History of New York City to 1898*.

Pg. 484. Robinson, Solon, *Hot Corn: Life Scenes In New York Illustrated: Including The Story Of Little Katy; Madalina, The Rag-Pickers Daughter; Wild Maggie, Etc.* Pg. 70. Sante, Luc, *Low Life: Lure and Snares of Old New York.* Pgs. 28–29.

3. A *taildiver* is a pickpocket.

4. William Henry Lane was a black dancer known as Master Juba, who along with Irish dancers probably invented tap dancing. See: Anbinder, Tyler, *Five Points: The 19th Century New York City Neighborhood that Invented Tap Dance, Stole Elections, and Became the World's Most Notorious Slum.* Pgs. 172–175. *(n.b. Lane is described in Anbinder's book as being 16 years old when seen by Charles Dickens in 1841. In 1838, the time of our story, he would have been 13 years old, perhaps at the start of his career.)*

5. Shirt tailer, a member of a gang called the Shirt Tails, who operated in the Five Points area and wore their shirts outside their trousers. See: Asbury, Herbert, *The Gangs of New York; An Informal History of the Underworld.* Pgs. 20–21.

6. Arcade and Diving Bell Saloons. Two saloons located on Orange Street in the first illustration of a map of Five Points, 1830–1854. See: Anbinder, Tyler, *Five Points: The 19th Century New York City Neighborhood that Invented Tap Dance, Stole Elections, and Became the World's Most Notorious Slum.* Pg. *ix.*

7. *(n.b. The author has associated Big Sue with a woman known as Rose Butler; a black servant who, in 1820 was convicted of arson, and publicly executed in potter's field a place that would become Washington Square.)* See: Burrows, Edwin G., and Mike Wallace, *Gotham: A History of New York City to 1898.* Pg. 506.

8. The Old Brewery was a converted brewery turned into a notorious house of ill repute—what some have called the worst example of degradation in all of New York. In fact, it was a place where the poorest and in some cases extra-legal people in Five Points found shelter and in many instances operated illegal speakeasies, grog shops and bordellos. It is mentioned in almost all histories of Five Points. See, Anbinder, Tyler, *Five Points: The 19th Century New York City Neighborhood that Invented Tap Dance, Stole Elections, and Became the World's Most Notorious Slum.* Pgs. 67–71. See also, Asbury, Herbert, *The Gangs of New York; An Informal History of the Underworld.* Pgs. 12–18. See also, Burrows, Edwin G., and Mike Wallace, *Gotham: A History of New York City to 1898.* Pgs. 476, 486, 747. See also, Foster, George G., *New York by Gas-Light.* Pgs. 121–122. See also, Mission, Ladies of the, *The Old Brewery and The New Mission House at Five Points.* Pgs. 33, 47–49. See also, Ottley, Roi and William J. Weatherby, eds., *The Negro In New York: An Informal Social History, 1626–1940.* Pgs. 76–77. See also, Sante, Luc, *Low Life: Lure and Snares of Old New York.* Pgs. 26–28.

Notes to Chapter Five

1. For a good discussion of dog and rat fights, see, Sante, Luc, *Low Life: Lure and Snares of Old New York.* Pgs. 106–107. See also, Burrows, Edwin G., and Mike Wallace, *Gotham: A History of New York City to 1898.* Pg. 486, and Ottley, Roi and William J. Weatherby, eds., *The Negro In New York: An Informal Social History, 1626–1940.* Pgs. 79–80.

2. In the 1830s slave catching and thwarting it were thriving businesses. See, Burrows, Edwin G., and Mike

Wallace, *Gotham: A History of New York City to 1898*. Pgs. 561–562. See also, Harris, Leslie M., *In The Shadow Of Slavery: African Americans in New York City—1626–1863*. Pg. 208.

3. Slumming was a habit of well-to-do New Yorkers of visiting Five Points to gawk at its poverty and displays of vice. It is said the practice was made fashionable by Charles Dickens' visit to the Points in 1841, however the habit began to grow during the 1830s. See, Anbinder, Tyler, *Five Points: The 19th Century New York City Neighborhood that Invented Tap Dance, Stole Elections, and Became the World's Most Notorious Slum*. Pgs. 32–34.

4. Bandog is a breed raised to be guard dogs, bloodlines from mastiffs.

5. Most women of the night or prostitutes took grandiloquent names. See, Foster, George G., *New York by Gas-Light*. Pgs. 97, 166.

Notes to Chapter Six

1. See, Anbinder, Tyler, *Five Points: The 19th Century New York City Neighborhood that Invented Tap Dance, Stole Elections, and Became the World's Most Notorious Slum*. Illustration Pg. 70. Brennan Company. name taken from this illustration of the Old Brewery which dates from 1850. *(n.b. Author believes the Brennan Company existed during the 1830s.)*

2. Leatherheads, a name given to Watchmen because of the leather helmets they wore. See, Burrows, Edwin G., and Mike Wallace, *Gotham: A History of New York City to 1898*. Pg. 636.

3. *Long Ago*, a popular song of the period. See Internet Sources. Nelson, Lesley aka *Contemplator's Popular*

Songs In American History Website. Early 1800s to Civil War.

Notes To Chapter Seven

1. For a fairly complete description of the Colored Orphan Asylum and its work, see, Harris, Leslie M., *In The Shadow Of Slavery: African Americans in New York City—1626–1863.* Pgs. 145–169.
2. Hackneys and Landaus are 19th Century carriages. See Internet Sources. Hoppe, Michelle, *Transportation in the 19th Century.* (LiteraryLiaisons.com/article033.html).
3. *[Quote]* 'In 1793 a federal Fugitive Slave Act was passed that stated that anyone claiming that a person residing in the North was a runaway from the South had only to appear before a local magistrate, personally or represented by counsel and submit proof of ownership.' *(n.b. Anyone who aided a fugitive was guilty of breaking a federal law and could be arrested and prosecuted.)* See, Burrows, Edwin G., and Mike Wallace, *Gotham: A History of New York City to 1898.* Pg. 560. *(Author's note:* Frederick Douglass, after writing the first edition of his Narrative, explained that to reveal the names of all who helped him would have put them in danger.)

Notes on Frederick Douglass

† In each narrative of the life of Frederick Douglass, he describes a scene where he meets an old friend who is so afraid of being discovered as a fugitive, he can hardly speak to Frederick. *(Author has described the scene differently to give nothing away to the reader before the revelation at the end of the story.)* See, Blight, David W., ed., *Narrative of the Life of Frederick Douglass: An American Slave, Written by Himself with Related*

Documents. See also, Douglass, Frederick, *The Essential Frederick Douglass: An African-American Heritage Book,* and McFeely, William S., *Frederick Douglass.*

†† Reverend Pennington is mentioned as being at his wedding in every version of Frederick Douglass' narrative of his life. While a man named Stewart is not mentioned as being at the wedding, Douglass mentions that it is a man named Stewart whom he meets outside of the Tombs Prison after several days of avoiding being captured *(the time of our story),* that eventually takes him to David Ruggles. See all of the above.

BIBLIOGRAPHY

1. Anbinder, Tyler. *Five Points: The 19th Century New York City Neighborhood that Invented Tap Dance, Stole Elections, and Became the World's Most Notorious Slum.* New York, 2001.

2. Asbury, Herbert. *The Gangs of New York; An Informal History of the Underworld.* New York, 1927.

3. Blight, David W., ed. *Narrative of the Life of Frederick Douglass: An American Slave, Written by Himself with Related Documents.* New York, 2003.

4. Burrows, Edwin G., and Mike Wallace. *Gotham: A History of New York City to 1898.* New York, 1999.

5. Dickens, Charles. *American Notes for General Circulation. In Two Volumes.* London, 1842.

6. Douglass, Frederick. *The Essential Frederick Douglass: An African-American Heritage Book.* Virginia, 2008.

7. Foster, George G. *New York by Gas-Light and Other Urban Sketches.* New York, 1850.

8. Harris, Leslie M. *In The Shadow Of Slavery: African Americans in New York City, 1626–1863.* Chicago, 2003.

9. McFeely, William S. *Frederick Douglass*. New York, 1991.

10. Mission, Ladies of the. *The Old Brewery and The New Mission House at Five Points*. New York, 1854.

11. Ottley, Roi and William J. Weatherby, eds. *The Negro In New York: An Informal Social History, 1626–1940*. New York, 1967.

12. Robinson, Solon. *Hot Corn: Life Scenes In New York Illustrated: Including The Story Of Little Katy; Madalina, The Rag-Pickers Daughter; Wild Maggie, Etc*. New York, 1854.

13. Sante, Luc. *Low Life: Lure and Snares of Old New York*. New York, 1991

INTERNET SOURCES

Bell, Philip A. (Speaker). *"Weekly Advocate"* (1837). Article by David Ruggles: *Beware Of Kidnappers*. (Doc #10536) 01685edi.pgs.1&2. University of Detroit Mercy—Black Abolitionist Archive.

Hodges, Graham Russell. (Spring/Summer) "David Ruggles: The Hazards Of Anti-Slavery Journalism," *Media Studies Journal, 14*, (2).

Hoppe, Michelle J. *Transportation in the 19th Century*. (LiteraryLiaisons.com/article033.html)

Nelson, Lesley aka *Contemplator's Popular Songs In American History Website*. Early 1800s to Civil War.

Osofsky, Gilbert—Source: The Journal of American History, Vol. 55, No. 2 (Sep., 1968), pp. 243–255 The Enduring

Ghetto Author(s): Published by: Organization of American Historians. *(Pg. 244, footnote #2)*

Palmer, A. Emerson, M.A. *The New York Public School: Being a History of Free Education in the City of New York.* New York, 1905. *Google Books.*

Ruggles, David. *Emancipator* (1836). Speech delivered recounting experience of Eliza Drummings, etc. *Traitors Exposed.* (Doc #01354). University of Detroit Mercy—Black Abolitionist Archive.

ACKNOWLEDGMENT

I WOULD LIKE TO THANK my friend Dr. Molefi Asante, PhD., my sister, Charlotte Jahn, and cousins Rachel Slaughter, MA and Marguerite Tigg Birt, Ed.D who gave this story its first read and encouraged it forward.

THE AUTHOR

CHARLES FULLER is the author of *A Soldier's Play* and the 1982 recipient of the Pulitzer Prize for Drama, Best American Play, New York Critics Circle Award, Edgar Allen Poe Award for Mystery Writing and the 1985 Academy Award Nominee for Best Screenplay for the motion picture *A Soldier's Story*. After a long history in theatre and film, *Snatch: The Adventures of David and Me in Old New York, Volume 1*, is Mr. Fuller's first venture into the world of children's books.